ALSO BY EMILY MIMS

The Smoky Blues series

Mist

Smoke

Evergreen

Indigo

Emerald

Mistletoe

Violet

Ruby

Amethyst

Noelle

The Texas Hill Country series

Solomon's Choice

After the Heartbreak

A Gift of Trust

Daughter of Valor

Welcome Home

Unexpected Assets

Never and Always

A Gift of Hope

Once, Again

Other Romances

Season of Enchantment

A Dangerous Attraction

For the Thrill of It All

VIVI'S LEADING MAN

Durango Street Theatre – Book 1

Emily Mims

www.BOROUGHSPUBLISHINGGROUP.com

VIVI'S LEADING MAN

ISBN 978-1-948029- 90-2

ACKNOWLEDGMENTS

Thanks to the Boroughs art department for a terrific cover. Many thanks to the Boroughs editors for making me look better than I am. Edwin Floyd, you are the best beta reader ever.

And a special shout-out to all the folks at San Antonio's Woodlawn Theatre for opening your theater and your hearts to me for the Durango Street Theater series! The Woodlawn Theatre is a San Antonio treasure, and Charles and I feel privileged to be part of the Woodlawn family.

VIVI'S LEADING MAN

Prologue

November

Miguel leaned against a support column at the back of the darkened Durango Street Theater and watched with hooded eyes as the Wicked Witch terrorized Dorothy and Munchkinland. Tonight was the last night that Dorothy and her ragged band of followers would triumph over the Wicked Witch and her minions, but posters in the lobby proclaimed the imminent opening of the Durango's Christmas production of *Joseph and the Technicolor Dreamcoat*, as well as posters advertising the first three productions scheduled for the new year. The Durango did six musicals a year, and had something either in production or on stage for much of the calendar year. It was one of the busiest theaters in town and enjoyed critical acclaim along with success at the box office.

Like he gave a damn.

Not that he didn't enjoy a good stage performance, and he had to admit, the Durango had a more than competent troupe of actors. If his memory served, the girl playing Dorothy and the boy playing the scarecrow had acted opposite one another often in the last three years. Glenda the Good Witch looked familiar, but he couldn't quite place her. However, he was drawn over and over to the tall woman who was all over her role as the Wicked Witch, owning the stage with every line she delivered. Hands down, she was the best actor up there, easily besting the tiny dark-haired child playing the head Munchkin, and the damned dog playing Toto.

Vivienne Heiser was a damned fine actress. One of the best in the city. She'd excelled in every role she'd ever played. Except for one.

She hadn't done such a great job as his wife.

Hence the divorce that had been finalized back in the spring. The divorce they'd been convinced they wanted.

The divorce he was beginning to regret.

Hell, he regretted it ten minutes after he'd agreed to it.

Glenda waved her arms and the Wicked Witch vanished in a cloud of smoke. With Vivienne off the stage, Miguel's interest in the production disappeared. He watched a couple more minutes before slipping from the auditorium. He looked around the lobby, noting the faded carpets needed replacing, and the dingy paint job on the walls.

He found the stairs to the balcony and slipped into an unsold chair on the aisle. He had a perfectly good paid-for seat downstairs, but he didn't want Vivienne or any of her theater buddies to see him tonight. Not that any of them except Vivienne would recognize a tattooed dude in a ball cap sporting a three-day beard as the usually clean-shaven ex-husband who had graced their society friend's arm for the better part of three years.

Still, he didn't feel like taking the chance that any of them would place him. He hadn't come tonight to check out his ex-wife's performance. No, tonight he was visiting the property itself, here at the behest of Vivienne's beloved Uncle Joe. Miguel was surreptitiously checking out the old theater to ascertain the value of the building and the land it sat on.

Good thing the Wicked Witch didn't know. Never mind the monkeys. She'd come sailing over that balcony after him.

Which was not how he wanted their first encounter after the divorce to go.

But he would like to see her again. Preferably between the sheets of his king-size with her legs wrapped around his hips as she came in his arms.

Miguel shifted uncomfortably in the narrow seat. Damn, he missed her in his bed. Although their marriage hadn't been a love match, the sex had been phenomenal. So much so that they were able to gloss over their fundamentally different outlooks on life until the knot was tied. Even after their differences surfaced, they'd struggled for three years before throwing up their hands in defeat and hired lawyers.

And absolutely breaking her dying father's heart.

Miguel swallowed the lump that always clogged his throat when he thought of Tripp Heiser. Not able to stand being in the theater another minute, Miguel pushed himself out of the chair and took the stairs down to the lobby two at a time before heading out onto Cesar

Chavez, the avenue that had once been called Durango Street. If his eyes were a little wet no one would notice under the ball cap.

The street and the sidewalks were clogged this time of night with the eclectic mix of natives and the tourists who flocked to downtown San Antonio. The November evening was perfect with a near full moon suspended in the inky sky, and air balmy enough for his short-sleeved T-shirt. He walked a half block to his favorite dive bar, the one he'd frequented as a kid from the west side when he'd wanted to shake off his ambition for the evening and be Mico. He slid onto a bar stool and ordered a Corona. The bartender shoved the requisite lime in the bottle and pushed it toward him. "Here's to you, Tripp," Miguel murmured as he held up the bottle in a salute to the mentor who'd meant so much to him.

Miguel nursed the beer, cursing the memories that chased around in his head like squirrels on a tree trunk. Tripp had seen something in the ambitious kid from the west side barrio and taken him under his wing, arranging an internship with Heiser Steel during Miguel's senior year of high school, then later, pulling the strings that would get him a scholarship to the San Antonio branch of the University of Texas. Tripp had offered Miguel a job before he graduated college, but had taken Miguel's refusal in good grace and instead loaned him seed money to buy his first fixer-upper. Tripp had been there for Miguel with Coronas and advice over heaping plates of enchiladas and chile rellenos at the café next door to Heiser Steel and acted as proud as a father could have been when Miguel made his first million.

He sipped the rapidly warming beer and wondered if Tripp had been playing matchmaker that afternoon five years ago, when he'd included his daughter, Vivienne, at one of their regular lunchtime get-togethers. Vivienne had always thought so. They were hardly one another's type. With Miguel's taste for sweet, shapely Latinas from his old neighborhood, and Vivienne subjected to the steady diet of society boys her mother had paraded through the house, they didn't have any common ground. But a small kernel of interest had prompted him to ask her out and, surprisingly, she'd accepted. Their first outing was to a reception given by one of her father's banker friends. Miguel expected to feel like a fish out of water and instead met a roomful of key players in the San Antonio financial community, three of whom were interested in doing business with the up-and-coming "West Side Wunderkind," as Tripp had so kindly dubbed him. Miguel had known Vivienne ran in circles that he'd never aspire to on his own. It didn't take him long to snap to the fact that an alliance with her would grant him entry into her circle. She could open doors for him that would be locked to the west side boy otherwise, no matter how successful his business became.

Miguel tossed back the rest of his beer and left enough on the bar for the drink and a generous tip. He smiled grimly as he exited the familiar dark space for the busy sidewalk. He didn't know whether to linger downtown or head back to his high-rise condo where he lived alone these days. The condo he'd bought to keep his wife in the lifestyle she'd enjoyed, including clothes, cars, and nice vacations. Pretty much whatever money could buy. Those were his contributions to the partnership—his money for her class and social connections.

It should have been a match made in financial heaven.

Hadn't turned out that way.

Miguel headed toward the parking lot. The sidewalk took him back by the Durango. He looked at the old building and curled his lip. Right there sat a lot of what had gone wrong in his marriage. He'd known before they were married that she loved acting at the old theater. But he hadn't realized what an obsession it was for her and her brother Cameron until Miguel was living with her and putting up with the crazy production schedules. Endless hours rehearsing. Dead week. Three performances a week for two months. Then she would land another role and the cycle would start all over again. And she did it all for free. She didn't earn a fucking penny for all that time and effort.

At first he'd tried to understand. Then he'd called her on it, only to be hit with the accusations. "Why should I give it up so I can spend more time with you when you're not here anyway?" she'd yelled during one of their epic battles. "You're off on a job site or schmoozing in a restaurant with a new client until nine or ten every damn night. I'd rather be at the theater than sit here by myself. Besides, I'm doing some good at the Durango. I'm bringing theater to families who'd never have it otherwise. You're only chasing a buck."

Oh, yeah. They'd sharpened their tongues on one another on too many occasions to count. She was impractical and idealistic. He was crass and money-grubbing. She was a dreamer. He was an ass.

Now they were divorced.

And in the hours after midnight, when sleep eluded him as it often did these days, Miguel knew down to his bones that he missed her. He missed her stuff in the bathroom, the conversations over coffee in the morning, the wild sex they'd reveled in until their passion had turned into anger.

And true, he missed her business connections.

Miguel found his Lexus, put down the top and threw his ball cap on the seat. The wind felt good in his hair as he sped down the expressway. He swallowed back the what-ifs that had plagued him since the divorce and forced himself to think about things as they were now.

His mentor was gone and his marriage to Vivienne was over. Vivienne and Cameron were trying to run Heiser Steel. *Trying* was the operative word. Gossip had it that Heiser Steel was in trouble. Big trouble. And had been since long before Tripp died.

Uncle Joe had hopes that he could help them save it. The old man, whose days were numbered, had hatched a plan to save Tripp's company and his family, and at the same time effect a possible reconciliation between Miguel and Vivienne. He laughed as he took the exit to his condo. They didn't have a snowball's chance in hell of reconciliation, especially once Vivienne knew the theater property would have to be sold. She would never forgive him or Joe for the loss of her beloved Durango Street Theatre.

Not that Miguel pointed that out to a dying man. But the sacrifice of the theater would be worth it if it saved Heiser Steel. And Miguel would make damned sure Heiser Steel was saved.

He owed that much to Tripp Heiser, Vivienne's feelings be damned.

Chapter One

January

Vivienne stepped back from the bathroom mirror and cast a practiced eye on this morning's makeup job. Beige and nude eye shadow highlighted her hazel eyes. A few swipes of mascara on her lashes, and a bit of blush graced her sharp cheekbones. Barely there lip-gloss coated her too-thin lips. Skillfully applied and subtle, it was perfect for the offices of Heiser Steel and nothing like the stage makeup she painted on when she took to the boards at the Durango, or the sophisticated face she wore when attending one of San Antonio's endless social occasions as a scion of the Heiser Steel Company.

Not that the cosmetics really mattered. No makeup job in the world was going to turn her plain face into a thing of beauty. She looked too much like Tripp Heiser to ever be accused of being beautiful. Sure, she could make herself attractive, and she was vain enough to care what she looked like.

But, she was a Heiser, which meant she didn't have to be beautiful. It didn't matter one bit what she looked like. Not when the Heiser family had belonged to the upper crust of San Antonio society for five generations, ever since her grandfather's grandfather founded Heiser Steel in 1892 and the company had enjoyed booming financial success for over a century.

Success it wasn't enjoying too much of today.

Which went a long way toward explaining the shadows beneath her eyes and the tension tightening her lips. Sighing, she ran a brush through her stick-straight shoulder-length hair and tucked it behind her ears. She leaned into the mirror. Light brown roots were beginning to show above the ash blonde highlights, but she could go at least another two weeks, maybe even a month, before she had to make another trip to the salon where she'd be fussed over and coddled.

Thankfully business attire in San Antonio was a bit more relaxed than in larger cities, allowing her to get away with colorful mixing and matching. Today's combination was a navy pencil skirt and red blouse, both expensive relics from the days when Miguel was paying for her wardrobe, and both seen recently in other combinations.

Pushing those thoughts aside, she shoved her feet into a four-year-old pair of Christian Louboutins and picked up her vintage Burberry bag. She glanced at the alarm clock. She had enough time for one more cup of coffee to combat the effects of yet another night of tossing and turning and dreaming of bottom lines printed in red. She strode into her miniscule kitchen and popped a pod in the expensive coffeemaker she'd snagged on her way out of the spacious condo she'd shared with Miguel.

She looked around at the tiny one she lived in now—a fraction of the size of her former digs, and a good twenty years older. At least it was in fashionable Alamo Heights, the posh neighborhood preferred by San Antonio's old-money crowd, where she'd grown up and her parents and grandparents had grown up before her. Her home had the dubious distinction of being a few doors down from the larger condo her mother and Aunt Katie had shared since her mother had been forced to sell the sprawling stone house where Vivienne and her brother Cameron had grown up. The proceeds from the sale had bought a few months of breathing room for Heiser Steel, and had left her mother with the illusion that all their financial problems were solved.

Which they weren't. Not by a long shot.

Speaking of, Vivienne grimaced at the light tap on the front door signaling another early morning visit. Which of the clueless sexagenarians would it be today? She hopped down off the barstool and threw open the door to find her cookie-cutter pretty, smiling mother, already dressed to the nines for her Tuesday morning gig as a museum docent. Vivienne couldn't think of more than one or two occasions when Betsy Heiser had looked less than perfect. Her mother had always been, and still was, a hard act to follow in that regard.

"Good morning, darling. Headed for work or the theater?"

Vivienne's mouth tugged into a smile. "The office. The theater's dead until noon. I'll go by there after work."

"You should. The theater makes you and Cameron so happy."

Vivienne moved aside. "Come on in. We can have coffee before you head out for the museum."

Her mother followed her into the kitchen and perched on a barstool. Vivienne handed her mother the brewed cup and made another for herself. Her smile fading, Betsy eyed Vivienne thoughtfully as she sat down on the other stool. "I thought we agreed you were going to get a few more items to augment your wardrobe. You've been wearing the same things since you and Miguel separated. And it's time to make an appointment with Claudette."

Vivienne refrained from rolling her eyes. Barely. "Mom, there's no money for new clothes right now, or a trip to the salon. Cameron and I are barely drawing enough salary for food and rent."

"Why, that's nonsense. We sold the house last year like Cameron said we should. There's plenty of money."

"No, Mom, there isn't. We bought a few months of floating, and that's about over. Heiser Steel's in as much trouble as it ever was."

"But we sold the house for over seven million dollars."

"Mom, you're forgetting that Dad refinanced it when the business got in trouble a few years back. We didn't see anywhere near that much money when it sold."

Betsy flicked her hand in a shooing motion. "You and Cameron worry too much. Everything's going to be fine. It's Heiser Steel. It's been here forever. It'll be here forever."

Vivienne bit her lip. There was no point in arguing with her mother. Betsy wasn't going to accept that fact that Heiser Steel was in trouble until they were out on the street, and maybe not even then. Vivienne changed the subject and until their coffee was gone listened to her mother's juicy tidbits about San Antonio's elite. They walked down the stairs to the garage where Betsy's two-year-old Lincoln was parked next to the Beamer convertible Vivienne had gotten in the divorce. "It's about time for new cars, don't you think?" her mother asked brightly. "For both of us."

"Next year," Vivienne replied through clenched teeth. *And probably not even then.*

Betsy eyed the cars doubtfully. "If you say so, dear." She air-kissed Vivienne. "See you."

Then Betsy hopped into the Lincoln, her smile bright as she headed out.

Vivienne followed more slowly, the tension in her head and neck promising a headache by noon. She understood where her mother was coming from all too well. Betsy Pennington Heiser had been born into the lap of luxury and had brought considerable wealth into her marriage to Heiser heir Cameron Gunther Heiser III. Betsy knew in her head that most of that wealth was gone now, having been used to prop up Heiser Steel when it had floundered fifteen years ago. But her mother simply couldn't understand that no money meant the luxuries she'd taken for granted all her life were no longer hers to enjoy. Aunt Katie, her father's sister, was equally as broke and no less out of touch with the family's current financial reality. Vivienne and Cameron had done a better job of adjusting. They were realists. They understood what had happened years ago when their father began trying to save an industry that had been sourced overseas for cheaper material made in countries where the labor force worked for pennies on the U.S. dollar.

Plus, Vivienne had bitter memories of the disaster her marriage her turned into. When one married solely for financial reasons there was nothing holding the couple together. She and Miguel had been the poster children of incompatible, and she had no desire to go there again.

Out on the street was better than that.

Rush-hour traffic clogged the expressways as Vivienne inched her way across town to the industrial park that was home to Heiser Steel and other manufacturing companies. The unassuming metal building housing the factory and business offices was a far cry from the elegant homes her family had lived in for generations, but it was the heart and soul of Heiser Steel.

She parked her car next to Cameron's lovingly restored Shelby Mustang and entered through the back door straight into the fabrication area, where their team of dedicated metalworkers were already busy cutting, assembling, and welding together the components for a variety of construction projects.

At one time Heiser Steel had been the go-to steel fabrication company for most of Texas, but stiff foreign competition, combined with her grandfather's inexplicable refusal to grow the business in the seventies and eighties, had seriously limited their market. Her father's attempt to expand in the nineties had been a financial disaster. Cameron's insistence on widening their scope from all-industrial fabrication to smaller, custom projects like hotel light fixtures and furniture had yet to pay off, although her brother was firmly convinced that it would eventually.

If the company lasted that long.

But it was hard to argue with Cameron when he was willing to do the custom designs and some of the welding himself. She ignored the screeching assault on her hearing and spotted him at the work station he'd recently installed, looking nothing like her usually expensively dressed, sophisticated brother under the hard hat, welding mask, ear protectors, work clothes, and steel-toed boots.

He was fashioning a set of custom light fixtures for a fancy Riverwalk restaurant's remodel, and even across the factory floor Vivienne could tell the lights were exquisite. Cameron spotted her and nodded. She threw up her hand in a wave and left him and the others to it, making her way to the office that was her purview. Their faithful receptionist and secretary had retired last month and she and Cameron had been in no hurry to replace her, choosing to split Mrs. Hernandez's responsibilities for the time being. Vivienne tackled today's emails first and was in the process of writing up a bid for a Hill Country construction project when the phone rang. "Is this Vivienne Heiser?" a chirpy voice asked. "Mr. Solomon wanted me to call and remind you of your two o'clock meeting with him today. He was afraid it would slip your mind."

Damn. She *had* forgotten. "Tell Mr. Solomon I'll be there."

Vivienne sighed as she hung up. Eloy Solomon was her late Uncle Joe's attorney. Joe Lang had been her father's college roommate and best friend and she'd loved him as family. She wondered, not for the first time, what was so important that she had to go in for a meeting with his lawyer. Probably a small bequest in his will. Or maybe a request. With Uncle Joe it could be anything.

Cameron trudged into the office about noon, covered in sweat. He pulled off the face mask and ear protectors and dumped his hard hat on his desk. "Got anything coming for lunch?"

"No, but we can grab take-out tacos next door."

"I'll buy."

"I'll let you."

Cameron returned fifteen minutes later with a deliciously aromatic sack. The *carne guisada* tacos were warm and Vivienne took a minute to slather hers with hot sauce. "Damn, that's good."

Cameron ate half of his in one bite. "So how's it coming on this end?"

"You know the answer to that as well as I do. It's sucky, Cam."

"Shit. Did you send off that bid for the Hill Country job?"

"Ten minutes ago. I gave them the absolute best price we could afford. I hope we can compete with that big company out of Houston."

Cameron swallowed the rest of his taco. "It's getting scary, Vivi. Five generations and I'll be the one to lose it."

"We—not you. But we can't take all the blame. Granddaddy and Daddy both made bad business decisions that are coming home to roost. Look at it this way. Most of the time it's the third generation that fucks it all up. Heiser Steel's made it two generations past that."

"If you say so." Cameron leaned back in his chair. "Jesus, I'd give anything if you were still married to Miguel."

Vivienne felt a hot spurt of anger. "That's a shitty thing to say. Tell you what. The next time one of us marries for money, it can be you."

"Fine. You drag San Antonio into the twenty-first century, then you can find me a rich guy into sexy welders. I'll marry him in a heartbeat," he responded.

Vivienne rolled her eyes and stuffed the rest of the taco into her mouth. She helped herself to a second and gathered up the trash from her desk. It was time to head out. It was after one already, and she didn't want to be late. She would find out what was so important that it required a face-to-face with Eloy Solomon, and then she would drop by the theater on her way back to the office, maybe hang out with Josh or Maggie or Rachel if they were there. Vivienne had always loved hanging out at the Durango. It had been her happy place for a long time, and with the divorce and all the troubles at Heiser Steel, it was the only happy place she had left.

She walked into Eloy Solomon's office right at the stroke of two. The gum-chewing, pink-haired receptionist motioned her to a chair. "Mr. Solomon's on an unexpected conference call. He said to apologize and tell you it will be about fifteen minutes."

Vivienne shrugged inwardly and sat down in the modest waiting area. She picked up a local rag and was looking through an article touting San Antonio's best tamale factories when the door opened and an all-too-familiar figure strode into the room. Vivienne stiffened in her chair and stared in shock at the broad-shouldered, good-looking businessman dressed in his favorite Ralph Lauren suit. Immediately her thoughts zoomed to how he looked coming out of the shower, water dripping from his straight dark hair and those broad shoulders, dressed in nothing more than a come-hither smile. Her breath hitched in her throat.

What is Miguel doing here? She hadn't seen him since the divorce.

He looked at her and his eyes widened. But not with surprise. Aggravation, maybe. Or some other emotion she didn't have the energy or desire to place.

Miguel turned away from her. "I'm here for my two o'clock meeting with Mr. Solomon," he told the receptionist quietly, totally ignoring Vivienne.

Which was fine by her. She had no desire to talk to him, either.

He was given the same explanation she'd gotten. Miguel didn't try to hide his irritation as he sat down across from her and picked up another copy of the magazine she held. Knowing Miguel, he was counting the minutes he would be gone from his precious construction company and inwardly cursing the time away from his desk. Vivienne's lips tightened. Why in the hell was her ex-husband here this afternoon? He'd only met Uncle Joe a handful of times.

Her interest in the magazine forgotten, she let herself take surreptitious peeks at her ex. The sight of him still made her heart beat a little faster. Miguel Abonce was as drop dead gorgeous as ever, with striking features. His broad forehead, high cheekbones, and square jaw set off a prominent chiseled nose. Wide, beautifully curved lips could curl into a beguiling smile or just as easily into a snarl. Straight hair as black as a raven's wing was expensively styled and the high-dollar suit concealed muscular arms and a broad, strong chest covered with the tattoos of his youth. He wasn't a particularly tall man, an inch or two shorter than she was, if the truth be known, but with his innate strength and the power of his presence, he commanded any room he entered. He moved with a natural grace that as an actress, she envied. He was one hell of a package, at least on the outside.

The inside was a vacant parking lot with an attendant taking money.

They continued to ignore one another until Mr. Solomon's door opened. He greeted them with a big smile. "Come on in, both of you."

"Both of us?" Vivienne asked. "Wouldn't it be better if you talked to us separately?"

"No. This concerns both of you and I'd rather go through it only once." Mr. Solomon motioned them into his office.

Both men motioned to Vivienne to lead the way. She took one of the chairs across from the desk and Miguel took the other. Mr. Solomon sat in his executive chair and then handed them both folders containing copies of Uncle Joe's will. "The part that pertains to the two of you starts on page seventeen."

She flipped to page seventeen and started reading at the point indicated by a sticky arrow. She read down the paragraph quickly at first, and then more slowly as what she read started to make an impact. Her heart began to pound in her throat as she read through the two pages for the second time, still trying to absorb the incredible truth spelled out in the document in front of her.

Uncle Joe had been the mysterious owner of the Durango Street Theatre and the building next to it that housed the Academy and theater offices. The theater folks had wondered for years who their shadowy landlord was, the topic fueling many a beery argument at their cast parties. She'd talked about it more than once with Uncle Joe, speculating that it could be any number of prominent San Antonians. He had speculated right along with her, postulating everyone from bank presidents to their current congressman.

The joke was on her. And the cagey bastard hadn't ever let on.

Now, to make matters worse, he had willed it jointly to her and Miguel.

What the hell?

She glanced over at Miguel, who didn't look surprised in the least. Vivienne's lips tightened. Crap. He had known about this already. "When did Uncle Joe tell you about this?" she asked accusingly.

"Back in November. I checked out the property the last night of *Wizard of Oz*."

"And nobody saw you? Oh, wait. I guess you were there in barrio boy mode."

Miguel's face tightened ever so slightly at the barb. "I might have let a few tattoos show that night. Anyway, the theater is a dump and the building next door is arguably worse. But the land it sits on is worth a mint. It ought to go for a pretty penny."

"Like hell it will," Vivienne snapped as she fisted her hands. "I'll never sell, and Uncle Joe knew that. And why you? Why did he leave half to you?"

"I bailed him out of a financial crisis a few years ago and he was never able to pay me back." Miguel hesitated a minute. "He sent me to the theater that night, Vivienne. He had every intention for us to sell it and for you to use your share of the money to bail out the company. He loved Tripp like a brother and wanted you and Cameron to be able to keep Heiser Steel."

"I. Am. Not. Selling." She could hear her voice rising and didn't care. "He wouldn't have left it to me if he wanted it sold."

"He did want it to be sold," Miguel said softly. "And sold it will be. Whether you like it or not."

"Guess again, Midas. It will be a cold day in hell before I sign one goddamn thing toward a sale, so you can shove it up your –"

Mr. Solomon cleared his throat. Loudly. "Uh, Miss Heiser, Mr. Abonce, let's not get ahead of ourselves. There is a caveat on the next page of the will that neither of you has seen yet. It won't make a difference in the long run, but it might postpone this argument for a few weeks."

Biting back her anger, Vivienne flipped to the next page. A smile played around her lips as she read the caveat. "Oh, this is precious. This is hilarious. We both have to participate fully in the next Durango Street production, from auditions to the closing night, before either of us can take possession. I love it." She looked at Miguel, who looked thoroughly put out.

"This is ridiculous. I don't have time for this bullshit." Miguel threw the will down on the desk. "Besides, it only prolongs the inevitable."

"Be that as it may, those are Mr. Lang's stipulations," Mr. Solomon told them. "You both have to participate in an entire production at the Durango. I will need an affidavit after the production is over signed by both the executive director and the chairman of the theater board that you each fulfilled that requirement. If either of you fails to do so, the property will automatically go to the other party, presuming that they fulfill the requirement."

"Not a problem for me. I have every intention of doing the next show anyway." Vivienne grinned.

"You do every fucking show they put on," Miguel snapped. "That's all you ever do. Maybe if you and Cameron spent as much time running Tripp's company as you do down at the damned theater, you wouldn't be about to lose it."

"And maybe your idol Tripp Heiser should have done a better job of upgrading equipment, competing in a global marketplace, and taking his head out of the sand during his tenure and not left Cameron and me a mess. But hey, it's more fun to blame us, isn't it?" she accused bitterly. "Please tell me you're not going to deign to come down to the theater and waste your precious time with us, so I get the Durango."

Miguel turned to Mr. Solomon. "I'll do the damned show. I could use the money." He pointed at Vivienne. "And so could she. Even if she's too thick-headed to understand."

"Wonderful, wonderful," Mr. Solomon said quickly before Vivienne could respond. "Bring me your affidavits after the production is finished, and we'll see about going forward then, depending on what you decide."

"It's already been decided. The Durango will not be sold," she stated. She rose and swept from the room, giving neither man a chance to reply.

Sell the Durango? She'd rather cut off her right arm.

She was in the parking lot before Miguel caught up with her. "You're being totally ridiculous," he snapped as she clicked open her car doors. "That property's worth a fortune."

"You're right. The theater's *priceless.*"

"It's a crappy old theater putting on a bunch of second-rate productions. *Dios*, Vivi. This is your golden opportunity. If that property goes for what I think it will, you can save the business that's been in your family for five generations. Doesn't that mean anything to you?"

"But at what price? You go ahead and call us crappy if you want to. *We* know better. We bring theater to people who wouldn't have it otherwise. We do a damned fine job and our productions are quality. And you're forgetting what the Academy does for the kids. That theater's worth everything."

"Even losing Heiser Steel?" he asked quietly.

Vivienne took a breath. "If that's what it takes, then yes. I'm not selling, Miguel. Get it through that hard head of yours."

Her hands trembled as she jerked open the car door and slammed it. Her heart pounded in her throat as she peeled out of the parking lot. Had she really meant what she'd said to Miguel? She wasn't sure. She'd spent the past year angsting over Heiser Steel, praying every night for a reprieve, a chance to get back on their feet and be successful again. And now she had one. But, God, what a price. Giving up the theater that was her heart and soul. Giving up the one thing in life that kept her sane, that kept her going through a loveless marriage and a divorce and the business woes that plagued her. Losing the theater would be losing a part of herself.

But so would losing Heiser Steel.

Vivienne sucked in a breath and took the entrance ramp to the expressway. There had to be a way to save them both. Right now, the most important thing was to present a determined front to Miguel. If he had the tiniest inkling that she had doubts—that she was thinking about selling even a little—he'd be on it like a duck on a june bug. She'd seen him do it more than once during their marriage, and she'd be damned if he'd do it to her.

She'd be strong and firm and get him to see things her way if it was the last thing she did. And for this she'd need allies. She flicked on her Bluetooth. "Get me Josh Goldstein." Josh was the executive director of the Durango—one of the few paid employees. This would affect him even more than it would her.

Josh picked up a moment later. "What can I do for you, pretty lady?"

"The shit's just hit the Durango Street Theatre's fan and we need to talk. Can you shake loose for dinner this evening?"

"Yeah, I guess so. The shit's hit the fan?"

"In a big way, and I don't want to talk while I'm fighting traffic on Loop Four-Ten. Meet me and Cam at seven. Noodles okay?"

"Noodles work. You want me to bring anybody?"

"Maggie and Rachel, if they're available. I'll call Cam."
She rung off with Josh and called Cameron next.
"Cam? You're not gonna believe what I just found out."

Chapter Two

Miguel watched with hooded eyes as Vivienne's Beamer raced down the access road toward the entrance ramp. His dick hardened even as aggravation clawed at his insides. *Hijole*, how could one woman make him so damned mad and turn him on at the same time? But she always had. Even at the end, when they didn't do much but yell at one another, he was hard for her at the same time they fought like hell. They'd finished more than one shouting match by tearing off each other's clothes and going at it like monkeys.

Maybe they could do that again a time or two before she got it through her head that selling the damned theater was the only option.

A big fat drop of rain hit his forehead, and then another. He jumped into his car, taking the expressway in the other direction from Vivienne toward the offices of Abonce Construction, located in a modest building north of downtown. He'd thought about moving to swankier digs, but every time he was tempted he heard Tripp's voice in his head: "Don't waste your money on appearances. The only person you're impressing is yourself." Miguel had heeded that advice and many other business pearls of Tripp's over the years. And not for the first time Miguel wondered how Tripp's advice had been so spot-on and yet Heiser Steel had hit the skids.

Miguel knew his crack to Vivienne had been below the belt. She and Cameron *had* inherited a mess. But she made him so damned mad, half the time he didn't know what was going to come out of his mouth until the venom had spewed forth and the damage was done.

He drummed his fingers on the steering wheel. Damn Joe Lang. Making Miguel work a production before he could take possession of the property was ridiculous in the extreme. It wasn't going to change his mind about the theater. The property had to go. He wanted his half of the money and Vivienne desperately needed hers. He didn't understand Joe, but he would play along and do the production. It wasn't like he had much choice.

He flicked on the Bluetooth button and called the Durango Street Theatre's box office. A cheerful voice he didn't recognize informed him that the next production was *Anything Goes* and that auditions would be held this coming Sunday. He wasn't about to audition for a part, but he would show up and volunteer to do something. He'd be damned if he'd give Vivienne or anyone else at the theater reason for that fucking affidavit to be denied.

The whole idiot bunch of theater people was as passionate about the place as Vivienne. Miguel shook his head. He didn't understand any of them. He sure as hell didn't understand his ex-wife. He hadn't expected her to be overjoyed at the loss of the theater, but to choose it over Heiser Steel? Moronic. That she'd be willing to sacrifice her family's business rather than lose the theater... he wasn't going to let that happen.

***

Josh Goldstein looked across the table of the small Asian bistro, disbelief on his face. "Please repeat that. I'm not believing what I'm hearing."

Vivienne swallowed a bite of pad Thai. "I know. It's incredible. Uncle Joe was the mysterious landlord we've speculated about for years. He left the theater to me and my asshole ex, who thinks he's going to sell it out from under me."

"*Hijole*," Maggie Gutierrez, the Durango's development director and fundraiser extraordinaire breathed. "Did you know he owned it ahead of time?" She absently swirled the stir-fried beef and noodles on her plate.

"No, she didn't," Cameron answered as he forked up a big bite of stir-fried chicken and snow peas. "And neither did I. I damned near dropped the phone when she called me this afternoon. The old bastard probably thought it was funny, keeping it a secret from everyone. Hell, he knew Vivi and I love the place."

"S'pose that's why he left it to you." Rachel Castillo stated. The artistic director looked down at her plate of stir-fried crispy chicken. "I don't know why I order this. It's not like I'm gonna like it."

"Why don't you pretend it's some of that fried chicken your Alabama grandma makes?" Vivienne grinned wickedly. "Or you could pretend it's one of your *abuela*'s flautas." Rachel had grown up eating the soul food of her African-American mother's family and the Tex-Mex dishes of her father's, and didn't like much else. "As to why he left it to me, asshole says Uncle Joe intended for me to sell it and use the money to save Heiser Steel. Supposedly Joe told him back in November."

"The big question is why he left the other half to the asshole," Josh asked as he wolfed down his moo goo gai pan.

"Miguel bailed him out of a bind a few years ago and Uncle Joe had never been able to pay him back," Vivienne replied.

"Doesn't sound like Miguel's that much of an asshole, not if he helped the man," Maggie said.

"Oh, he's an asshole all right. He complained constantly about the time I spent at the theater," Vivienne replied. "I don't know why he expected me to sit at home in the evenings and wait for him when he wasn't home either."

"Macho male," Rachel stated matter-of-factly.

"Ya think?" Vivienne snarked. "Anyway, we've about come to blows already. He thinks he's going to force a sale and I told him no way."

"I'm not an attorney, but it's my understanding that if you and Asshole inherited it jointly, he can't force you to sell it if you don't want to," Josh said.

"That's a relief," Vivienne breathed.

"But I'm not sure it solves any of your problems," Cameron told her. "Remember, there are expenses involved in owning a piece of prime downtown real estate. Taxes, upkeep, and so forth. And I promise you, the token rent we paid Uncle Joe sure wouldn't cover that."

"So why'd he keep it and rent it to us so cheap?" Maggie asked.

"Tax write-off would be my guess," Josh suggested. "The trouble with that is that you have to be rich enough to pay the property taxes before you can take it off your income taxes. Are you that flush?"

"I'm not, but Miguel is. Not that he's going to be willing to do that." Vivienne ran her hands down the sides of her face. "Dear God, why did Uncle Joe do this to me? Now I'm not only responsible for keeping Heiser Steel from going under, I have to find a way to save the Durango too." She pushed her plate away.

Cameron pushed the plate back in front of her. "Eat your dinner. Making yourself sick by not eating isn't going to accomplish a damned thing."

"Besides, you won't be going it alone in fighting to save the Durango. You have a whole theater full of people on your side," Josh said.

"Damn right." Cameron held up his hand and Josh high-fived him, a look of understanding passing between them.

Vivienne bit back a sigh. They would make a darling couple. It was a shame they were both involved with other people.

"We'll do anything and everything to keep the Durango going," Maggie stated firmly.

"We won't let you down," Rachel promised.

Vivienne felt the sting of tears. "Thanks, y'all. That means so much."

But what could they do, really? Vivienne wondered later as she drove through the chilly night toward her condo. Cameron was right. Sure, she could insist on keeping the place. But that would involve spending money she didn't have. And Miguel wasn't going to do a damned thing except push for a sale. Surely Uncle Joe expected her to keep the theater. He'd known how much it meant to her, and how big a part of her life it had been over the years. He'd have wanted her to keep it open. The theater was a San Antonio treasure.

And, hands down, it was the biggest source of joy in her life.

***

Miguel parked in the lot under the expressway and ambled down the sidewalk toward the Durango. A fresh norther had blown through in the wee hours of the morning, sweeping away the rain clouds that had lingered for the past week, leaving the air clear, the sky blue, and the winter sun bright. Food vendors were set up in Market Square for whatever festival was going on this weekend and the delicious aroma of grilling meat and frying onions wafted through the cold air, teasing his nose and making his stomach growl. He'd long since burned through the pan dulce he'd eaten at his home desk this morning while catching up on paperwork, so he veered off and detoured through the busy market, filled with tourists and San Antonians filling their stomachs and browsing the craft stalls. He shelled out for two jalapeno-laced sausages on a stick and a bottle of San Antonio's own Big Red soda, its sticky sweetness dulling the piquant burn of the jalapenos. He tossed the sticks and the empty bottle in the trash and headed toward the theater.

He wondered again for the thousandth time what in the hell Joe Lang thought he would accomplish by forcing Miguel to participate in a production before he could lay claim to his half of the theater. It wasn't going to change his mind. The theater would have to be sold. He'd not been happy to learn from his attorney that, since the theater was an inheritance and Vivienne was joint owner, he couldn't out and out force her to sell. But sooner or later the reality of the situation would sink in to his hard-headed ex. Owning a white elephant like the Durango would cost money. Money she didn't have, and money he wasn't coming up with. And she couldn't afford to have her credit sullied by a foreclosure any more than he could.

The front doors of the Durango were locked but he spied the tall young man who'd been Dorothy's scarecrow going in a side door, so he followed the actor into the back of the theater and down a short hall past what Miguel presumed was a dressing room. He looked around curiously, taking in the backstage area he'd never visited during his marriage to Vivienne.

The stage was bare without the set pieces associated with either their last show or their next one, although what looked like the makings of the next set were off to one side. The curtain was open and people were milling around in the orchestra pit and in the aisles. He found the stairs that would lead to the side aisle and wandered down, spotting several familiar faces he remembered from the performances he's seen and the cast parties he'd attended.

Vivienne's brother Cameron was his usual sophisticated self, dressed to the nines and seated on the front row holding a stack of papers. Although Cameron's appearances on the stage were few and far between, his role as board chairman had him down here almost as often as Vivienne. Miguel had gotten no sympathy the one time he'd complained to Cameron about Vivienne's devotion to the Durango. "You knew that when you married her," Cameron had told him tersely. "If it hadn't been for Heiser Steel, she would have majored in drama and performed on Broadway. So for God's sake, shut up about it and let her perform."

Miguel turned his attention from his former brother-in-law and spotted a good-looking young man he didn't know conferring with a gorgeous Hispanic woman a few years older than himself he thought was named Letti. They appeared to be in a heated discussion. Scarecrow boy sat down beside the pretty blonde who'd been Glenda and immediately began a lively conversation with her. Rachel Castillo, the artistic director, sat down beside Cameron with a stack of papers like his. Otherwise, the people gathered here today were strangers, which wasn't all that surprising. As his and Vivi's marriage had gone south, he'd spent less and less time with her and the theater crowd. Turnover rates for actors at the Durango were high, so it made sense that he wouldn't know too many of them anymore.

He slid into a chair and prepared to waste his afternoon watching the auditions. He wasn't about to try out for a part. He would do something else, take tickets or sell sodas or do something to fulfill the legal stipulation. That was all he had time for. He couldn't make it to the endless rehearsals. He couldn't sing or dance his way out of a paper bag, and he didn't think *Anything Goes* had any speaking-only parts. There was no way in hell he was getting up in front of San Antonio and making a fool of himself, as Vivienne so loved to do. But she didn't make a fool of herself up on that stage. She entertained her audience and did a damn fine job of it.

As pissed off as she made him sometimes, he had to admit that. She could sing and she could dance, and she could put on a show with the best of them.

The door to the side stairs opened and as always, his eyes were drawn to Vivienne as she glided down to the orchestra pit, smiling and waving to the scarecrow boy and Glenda woman. He hadn't seen or heard from her since their altercation at the attorney's office last week. Not that he'd expected to. He was certain that she too had consulted an attorney as to his ability to force her to sell. She probably considered it a victory for her and the theater. As far as he was concerned, it was only a minor setback.

As always, he stared at her as she sashayed down the aisle and sat down with the scarecrow and the good witch. Devoid of cosmetics and dressed in a pair of jeans and a tee with a picture of the Durango marquee on the front, she looked anything but an heiress or an accomplished actress. Her hair was pulled back from her face, making her features seem plain. Yet he couldn't seem to take his eyes off her. He didn't know what the hell it was about her that drew him so. He'd hoped the attraction would fade after the divorce, but now that they'd been thrown back together, it seemed to be getting stronger.

Whatever it was that was so compelling about the woman, he wished it would go away.

Rachel stood up and stepped to a microphone. "Anyone who hasn't filled out an audition sheet needs to do so before we get started. We need one from everyone, not only our actors. So everybody get out your pencils!"

He guessed that meant him.

Rachel started down the aisle passing out audition sheets and clipboards. He raised his hand and Rachel started toward him, her smile turning snarky when she recognized him under the unshaved face and the ball cap. "Hello, Miguel. Here to earn your half of Vivienne's theater?"

Okay. He knew where Rachel stood.

And from the looks he was getting from some of the others, they stood right there beside her.

Miguel was about as popular as a turd in the punchbowl.

He took the audition sheet and the clipboard, quickly scrawling the pertinent information and volunteering to usher or work in the lobby. He handed the clipboard back a few moments later. Rachel frowned and walked his sheet over to Cameron, who shook his head and wrote something else across it before handing it back to Rachel. Cameron got his phone out of his pocket, and a moment later a text message beeped on Miguel's phone.

Need to talk to you after auditions.

He started to get up to find out what Cameron thought was so important, but Rachel stepped up to the mic. "Ladies and gentlemen, it's time to hear you strut your stuff. I'm looking forward to seeing and hearing each and every one of you today." She beamed out at the auditioning hopefuls and looked down at the audition sheets in her hand. "Okay, I need Noel Flores, Jeannie Flynn, Heather Lopez, Mark Galvan, and Jody Parker. Let's get you up on the stage and see what you can do." She sat down on the front row with Cameron who was beside the young man Miguel didn't recognize.

He would have to wait until after the auditions to find out what Cameron wanted to say to him.

Whatever it was, he didn't expect it to be good.

***

Vivienne took a breath and smiled as she signaled Jerome at the keyboard. Their talented audition pianist launched into the intro of Cole Porter's famous "Anything Goes," the tongue-in-cheek tap tune decrying the modern world of the 1930s. As she went into the first verse, the lilting tune and catchy lyrics rolled off her tongue, and even though the audition didn't strictly require it, she went into an improvised tap dance during the instrumental bridges.

When the song was finished, she and Wade Baxter ran through a couple of pages of dialogue before she signaled Jerome to play "You're the Top." Satisfied that they'd knocked it out of the park, she and Wade held hands and bowed to their whistling, stomping fellow auditioners. Rachel smiled faintly and Josh and Cameron exchanged a look that she'd seen before and recognized.

Unless Sutton Foster and Colin Donnell of the Broadway revival were sitting in the audience waiting to audition, Vivienne and Wade had landed the roles.

They returned to their seats, neither of them giving in to the urge to smile and pump their fist. The last thing either wanted to do was to discourage a hopeful newbie. They needed those newbies for the chorus and to fill more challenging roles in productions to come. So they reined in their glee for the time being.

Besides, Wade wasn't too gleeful about anything these days. The young actress he'd performed with so often and lived with for nearly three years had taken her daughter back to Tennessee and reconciled with her singer husband, leaving Wade down a roomie or lover or whatever Sandra had been to him. And he missed Noelle, Sandra's little girl. Landing this role would help. Vivienne wasn't all that worried about Wade. He'd bounce back. She'd been hit a lot harder and she'd gone on with her life.

At least that's what she told herself.

Which is why it galled her that she kept sneaking peeks at her oh-so-compelling ex-husband, who was sitting across the theater with a pissed-off expression on his face. She was *over* Miguel.

Honestly she was. Besides, it wasn't like they'd married for love. He'd married her to gain access to her inner circle of San Antonio movers and shakers, and she'd married him so she could continue to enjoy the lifestyle she could no longer pay for herself.

And to enjoy the best sex she'd ever had.

Money and lust. The two worst reasons in the world to get married.

She dragged her gaze away from Miguel. She wouldn't make that mistake again. The next time she married, it was going to be for love. Period. Money wasn't going to be a factor.

But it would be more than a little all right if the sex was great.

Vivienne's lips twitched and she turned her attention back to the stage. Letti Aldrete was up there now and it was all Vivienne could do not to groan when Letti told Jerome to play the Hope Harcourt song "Goodbye, Little Dream, Goodbye." What in hell was Letti thinking? Hope Harcourt was the ingénue on this boat ride. The character was barely out of her teens and Letti was way too old for the role. She would have done better to audition for the part of Hope's mother. But no, the woman kept shooting herself in the foot by auditioning for roles that were fifteen or twenty years in her rearview mirror.

Letti sang the number and delivered a few lines. Rachel asked her if she would take any role they offered her and Letti shook her head. Vivienne barely stopped herself from rolling her eyes. Her friend had once again just lost out on being in a Durango production. She leaned over to Jessica Clary, who'd done a really great job with Glenda. "What did you put on your audition sheet?" Vivienne whispered.

"I said I'd do anything," Jessica whispered back.

"You should have specified Hope Harcourt. You need to sing that one when it's your turn."

"And risk Letti's wrath?"

"Letti won't give you a hard time," Wade said. "You're the one who casts her daughter. Letti's not gonna do anything to piss you off and jeopardize Sophie's status as queen of the teen productions." Wade didn't try to hide his cynicism. Jessica was the head of the Performing Academy and had total control over who was cast in lead roles in the youth productions. And Letti knew it.

"Except be the stage mother from hell." Jessica laughed. "Okay. I'll sing the 'Little Dream' song and hope for the best."

The auditions continued, and when it was her turn, Jessica did a beautiful rendition of "Goodbye, Little Dream, Goodbye," the poignant anthem to love and heartbreak. Her eyes were shimmering with tears as she bowed at the end. Vivienne bit her lip. Jessica was thinking about Robby again. It had been nearly five years and the young widow had yet to let go of losing her firefighter husband. Maybe someday she would be ready to embrace the future and let another man love her. But right now, not so much.

The auditions took the better part of three hours. Miguel had started shifting in his chair during the second hour, a surefire sign that he was getting impatient. Since he hadn't auditioned for a role, not that she'd in a million years expected him to, he would most likely be put on the crew. Vivienne bit back a smile at the thought. He was going to hate that. It was time-consuming and dirty, and there wasn't an ounce of glamor involved in taping the floor to place set pieces and moving sets between acts.

And he would be taking orders from the crew chief. Most likely Letti, since, once again, she'd insisted on a role she was too old to play. Letti was going to be pissed off and most likely grumpy with her crew. It had been awhile since Miguel had taken orders from anyone, and even longer since he'd had to put up with ill temper.

Vivienne snickered. This was going to be so much fun.

Miguel shot up out of his chair the moment the last audition ended. He marched over to Josh and Cameron. "Excuse me. I gotta see this up close," Vivienne said as she slid out of her seat. She'd seen Rachel's reaction to Miguel's audition sheet and the look on Miguel's face when he'd looked at his phone a moment later. She hot-footed it to the front, where Miguel stood with his arms folded, waiting impatiently for Rachel and Cameron to make notes on the last audition sheets.

Miguel finally cleared his throat. "I believe you wanted to talk to me?"

Cameron nodded. "In a moment," Rachel murmured.

Cameron finally looked up with the bland expression that usually meant he was about to deliver a bombshell. "It's about your audition sheet."

"What about it?" Miguel asked tersely. "I volunteered to either usher or work in the lobby. Is there a problem with that?"

"A big one," Rachel said. "We don't need you out there. Cameron and I think your talents would better serve us as a member of the crew."

"What does that involve? I only have so much time for this charade," Miguel half snarled.

"Your involvement would start the Sunday before the show opens. Tech week. I'm sure you've heard Vivienne talk about it," Cameron continued while staring at Miguel.

"I remember tech week all too well. Otherwise known as dead week. She disappeared for a fucking week." Miguel full-on snarled now.

"And this time you'll be disappearing right along with her." Rachel smiled at him. "You'll come in early that Sunday morning and will be expected to put in twelve to fourteen hours that day. Your presence will be required every night that week, and for three performances that weekend, as well as three performances a weekend for the next seven weekends. Come on, Mr. Abonce. You know all this. Why are you making us spell it out for you?"

"Because I don't have anywhere near that kind of time to waste. I said I would work the lobby or usher. That will have to do it."

"Actually, that won't do it at all," Cameron told him. "You want us to sign that affidavit, or don't you?"

"You must not want your half of this place all that badly," Vivienne interjected. "You go right on being an ass, Miguel. I'd love to own this place free and clear."

"And before you start sputtering about calling your lawyer and taking us to court, we've all read Vivi's copy of the will," Josh chimed in. When Miguel scrunched up his face, Josh said, "I'm Josh Goldstein." He grinned impudently and offered his hand. "I'm the new executive director, and while I'm not an attorney, I've read my fair share of wills and contracts. The will stipulates that you participate fully in an entire production. As a member of the crew you will do that. Out in the lobby you won't. It's that simple. Or if you'd rather, we can let you stumble around in the back of the ensemble. They start rehearsals next week. Tech week doesn't start for another month. What'll it be? The crew or the courtroom?"

Miguel's head snapped up. "Tell me, Mr. Goldstein. Did I say anything about taking any of you to court?" He looked at Josh derisively.

Josh's impudent grin faded. "No, you didn't."

He raked them all with a glare. "Did I say anything to anyone about lawyers, or court, or doing anything that would dishonor the memory of the man who owned this theater and rented it to you dirt cheap for years? That's not how I operate. I have more respect for Joe Lang and his legacy than that."

"Get down off your high horse, Miguel," Cameron warned. "We're merely trying to point out that in the spirit of Uncle Joe's wishes, you have to do more than usher or sell sodas. Obviously, he wanted you to learn a little something about what we do down here. I don't think serving on the crew is too much to ask."

"Fine. If you insist." Miguel pulled out his wallet and handed Josh his business card. "Email me a list of the dates and times I'm expected over here. And while you are emailing, Mr. Goldstein, I need copies of your financial records for the last three years. I need to know every building-related expenditure the theater and Mr. Lang incurred. And be sure you send copies to Vivienne. She needs to see them as well."

"I've already seen them," Vivienne said.

"Josh can get you the theater's paperwork," Cameron added. "You'll have to get Uncle Joe's records from his attorney."

"I'll be hearing from you, then." Miguel turned on his heel and took the side stairs to the stage door two at a time.

"My, that went well. He pulled off that insulted routine like a pro." Rachel snickered softly.

"No, he really was insulted," Vivienne explained. "Whatever else you may think about Miguel, he's honorable. He's the last businessman in town who would use the courts to get his way. Especially about something like this."

"You think he's honorable? He's trying to take the theater away from us," Josh protested.

"He is. But he's being up-front about it. Not trying to pull a fast one or lying to us about his intentions," Vivienne stated. "He's not soothing us into complacency so he can jerk the rug out from us. He's being totally transparent. Under these circumstances, not everyone would be."

"Whatever." Josh turned to Cameron. "So what about the documents he's asked for? Send 'em or stall?"

"Send 'em. Stalling accomplishes nothing." Cameron straightened the audition sheets in his lap. "And on that note, I'm out of here. I've got a wrought-iron gate calling my name and I can get more done when the shop's empty." He handed the audition sheets to Rachel and took off.

Rachel watched Cameron's exit. "Now, that's a fine figure of a man." She sighed wistfully. "What a waste."

Josh grinned impudently. "I don't think so."

Vivienne laughed. They bantered back and forth for a couple of minutes before she too left the building. She sailed out the back door, sliding to a halt when she spotted Cameron and Miguel in the parking lot across the street, standing beside Cameron's Mustang with their heads bent. The sight of them talking made her want to blow a gasket. Damn, was Miguel over there making the case to Cameron to sell the theater? Cameron loved the theater, but the possible loss of Heiser Steel weighed heavy on his shoulders. If it were up to him, she'd bet her grandmother's diamond brooch he would sell the Durango and save their company.

She started toward the men. Before she could get across the street, they shook hands and Miguel ambled toward the parking lot under the expressway. She marched up to Cameron, who was watching Miguel with hooded eyes. "So, has he managed to sweet-talk you into strong-arming me about a sale?"

"Ooh, Miguel's not the only one who's testy this afternoon." Cameron's eyes danced with amusement.

"If I am, it's no wonder. The bastard's out here trying to make his case and you're standing there letting him." Vivienne turned an accusing gaze on Cameron. "Well, did he succeed? Am I going to be subjected to a two-pronged campaign to divest myself of the Durango?"

"No, you're not going to be subjected to a campaign in any way, shape or form from me. I'm not listening to the likes of Miguel Abonce. He's out for himself and always has been."

"I'm glad you can see that. I didn't until it was too late." Vivienne sighed. "But he'll still be after me to sell."

"You better believe he'll be after you to sell. You can take it to the bank." He put his arm around her. "Now, I couldn't care less about what that asshole thinks, and am not falling for his arguments, persuasive though they may be. But I am going to say something you don't want to hear. I hope it doesn't come to pass, but sooner or later it may boil down to having to decide. And if it does, you need to think about what that infusion of cash could mean to Heiser Steel. It could make the difference in keeping the company or selling it."

"Yeah, that crossed my mind a few times. Like every thirty minutes last night between midnight and three. And again when I woke up again at seven. I'm all too aware of the reality facing us. I may not like the truth, but you can be damned sure that I'm well aware of it."

Chapter Three

Miguel rubbed his tired eyes and flicked on the turn signal of the company truck, veering off to the expressway exit that would take him to the home his mother and beloved *abuelita* shared. Thin gray clouds partially hid the late-morning winter sunlight, which was trying valiantly to peek through. He yawned and glanced down at the dashboard clock. It was almost eleven, a little earlier than he'd told Mama and *Abuelita* he'd be showing up. He'd finished at the Hill Country jobsite earlier than expected and thought it would be nice to have a cup of coffee in their cozy kitchen and talk with them while they finished making lunch. It would be good to talk to someone who didn't work for him.

He thought about how he and Vivienne would talk over dinner. Often she was at the theater, and when she wasn't, frequently he didn't come home from work in time to eat with her. But, when they did dine together, he'd enjoyed their banter. He wasn't above admitting that he missed their rambling conversations over steaks, or chicken, or Vivi's to-die-for spaghetti. They would tell each other about their respective days. Inevitably she would tell him the goings-on down at the theater. He would bounce ideas off her about his projects, and she would talk about Heiser Steel. They indulged in a bit of gossip from time to time. They'd flirt, which would lead to dessert in the bedroom.

Now it was takeout and paperwork until eleven or twelve.

He headed down a busy four-lane thoroughfare and into a beautiful older neighborhood about a mile north of the inner loop. Graceful live oak trees, still green with leaves even in the dead of winter, grew bent and gnarled between brick two-stories and sprawling sixties-era ranch houses.

He made two more turns and pulled into the driveway of a brick ranch house nestled between much larger homes. Miguel smiled at the red tricycle gracing the front porch. He'd bought that trike so his nephew Jeremy would have something to ride when Valerie and Sebastian brought him over.

Miguel hopped out of the truck and squeezed between the ancient Buick and much newer Camry parked side by side in the garage. He made his way through the pristine utility room into the warm kitchen, where he was greeted with the delicious aroma of tamales steaming on the stove, and a pot of pinto beans simmering on the back burner. The kitchen and breakfast nook were deserted, but he heard feminine voices coming from the family room. "Mama, you have to take your shot," he heard his mother say in Spanish. "Your sugar will go up if you don't."

"*Mija*, I'm tired of shots. Can't I use the pills like I used to?"

Uh-oh. *Abuelita* was feeling whiny today. Not that he blamed her. Two shots a day, every day, for the rest of her life was bound to get old. Miguel wondered when the dreaded diabetes would strike him. The Torres and Abonce clans were shot through with the disease, and a particularly virulent variety had taken his father, "Big Mike" Abonce, two weeks shy of his fortieth birthday, leaving Juliana Torres Abonce to raise her teenaged son and two school-aged daughters by herself. His grandmother Ximena, who'd also been widowed, moved in and joined forces with her daughter to raise him and his two younger sisters.

Miguel started a cup of coffee in the Keurig and went in search of his mother and grandmother. "*Hola, Mama. Hola, Abuela*," he called, automatically switching to Spanish. When he got to the family room, he leaned down and kissed his mother and a frowning grandmother. "Time to get your shot, *Abuela*. You wouldn't want to set a bad example in front of Jeremy, now would you?"

"*Esta bien*." *Abuelita* let her daughter pull up her sweater. As gently as she could, his mother gave the tiny old lady a shot in the fleshy part of her stomach. Grimacing a little, Ximena turned and smiled at Miguel. "You're early, *mijito*."

"Finished at the build site out at Canyon Lake sooner than I thought I would. Figured I'd come on over so you could catch me caught up on all the gossip."

Ximena frowned at him. "What gossip? Nothing ever goes on in this new neighborhood you insisted we move to."

"Which was exactly the point," his mother said dryly.

Ximena struggled to her feet, clutching her walker in a death grip. "I liked it better back in the old neighborhood. There was more going on."

"Sure was, *Abuela*," Miguel agreed. "All kinds of things. A shooting here, a drive-by there, the occasional drunken stabbing, not to mention gangs roaming the streets at three in the morning. Real fun, those things." His grandmother shot him a dirty look.

"Which is why Miguel bought this house and moved us here," Mama added tartly. "I love it here. We go to St. Agatha for Mass and to all the senior activities, so you get to see all your old friends."

"It's not the same. And it makes it harder for you to see Julio," *Abuelita* argued.

Mama shut her eyes and shook her head. His mother's gentleman friend had moved out of the barrio years ago and his grandmother knew it.

"Tell you what. Why don't we save this discussion for another time?" Miguel suggested. "I have coffee waiting for me in the kitchen, and you can tell me what the seniors of St. Agatha have been up to."

They got *Abuelita* settled at the kitchen table. Miguel sipped his coffee while his mother made a skillet of her wonderful Mexican rice. As he watched her skillfully chop onions and brown the rice, he wondered for the thousandth time if his parents would have made it out of the barrio if his father had lived. They were both excellent cooks. Big Mike had always dreamed of owning his own taco place, but died before he'd made it happen. "You can make your dreams come true, *mijo*," he'd said from his hospital bed as Miguel held his hand. "You work hard, you can do it." The dying man had squeezed his son's hand. "That way, you can take good care of your mama and your *hermanitas*. Promise me, Miguel."

He had lived up to his promise. He'd put Valerie through UT's nursing program and had sent Andrea to beauty school to follow her heart's desire. And, after years of badgering, he'd finally persuaded his mother and grandmother to move from the barrio to a nicer house in a safer neighborhood. Even though his grandmother found it boring, she knew she was better off here. And now that his mother had retired from her job at the small *taqueria* where she'd work for years, they could take care of each other, and he didn't have to worry nearly as much.

By the time lunch was ready, they had exhausted the St. Agatha gossip. Miguel's mouth watered when his mother set a plate loaded with *borracho* beans, rice, and homemade tamales in front of him. "What's with the tamales? Not complaining, but Christmas has come and gone." He inhaled appreciatively.

"She's making them for the neighbors," *Abuelita* said proudly. "The phone rings all the time with gringos wanting tamales for their parties."

"You selling them for enough to make a profit?" He popped a tamale out of the shuck and ate half in one bite.

"*Dios, sí.* I'm not getting rich, but it's fun and we have them all the time now, not only for Christmas." Mama unrolled a tamale. "The neighbors love them as much as Vivienne used to."

"She did love them, didn't she?" Miguel shoved the rest of the tamale in his mouth. "I saw her last week."

Both women's heads snapped up. "You did?" Mama asked.

"Where?" *Abuelita* demanded.

"At the lawyer's office, and then at the theater last Sunday." Miguel forked up a bite of rice.

"The theater? You hate that place," *Abuelita* said. "What were you doing there?"

"Long story short, Vivienne's Uncle Joe was the mysterious owner of the Durango. He left it to Vivienne and me with the proviso that she and I have to work an entire production before we can take possession. Then it's ours to do with as we wish. Unfortunately, we don't wish for the same thing."

"I'm surprised," *Abuelita* murmured.

"Let me guess. You want to sell it. She doesn't," Mama stated.

"That's putting it mildly. She swears she'll never sell, even if it costs her and Cameron Heiser Steel."

Mama tilted her head. "I didn't realize the company was in trouble again. I thought her *madre cabeza hueca* sold the mansion and they got back on sound footing."

Miguel snickered. Betsy Heiser was an airhead of the highest order. His mother had never had much use for his former mother-in-law. "It bought them some breathing room, that's all. They're barely hanging on by their fingernails. Joe left her half that theater so she could save her father's company. Not so she could grace the stage with her talent."

"Interesting. Why did he leave the other half to you?" *Abuelita* looked at him curiously.

"He owed me money. And, I'm guessing, because he knew I'd push Vivienne to sell."

"And you should. The girl has a responsibility to take care of her family," *Abuelita* said tartly.

"*Que tonteria,*" Mama snapped.

Abuelita raised a brow. "You think it's nonsense that she should take care of her family?"

"Who's to take care of? Vivienne and her brother could probably earn six figures or close to it in the business world. And Betsy Heiser's college educated and could go out and support herself. It's about time she did something besides look pretty and spend money."

Miguel's lips twitched. "Tell us what you really think, Mama."

Abuelita huffed. "But what about the family business? Isn't that important?"

"I certainly think so." Miguel rolled open another tamale. "It's a legacy. Her family's had it for five generations. I'm not sure she understands that."

"If she didn't understand it, she would be singing and dancing on Broadway, not stuck here in San Antonio running Heiser Steel." Mama laid her hand on Miguel's arm. "It's you who doesn't understand, *mijo*. Performing is everything to that girl. It feeds her soul. It would kill her to give it up."

Miguel's eyes narrowed. "So you think she should give up the company and keep the theater?"

"She gave up the marriage and kept the theater, didn't she?" *Abuelita* jabbed.

"And whose fault was that?" Mama shot back. "Hers, or the husband who refused to understand?"

Miguel looked at his mother in astonishment. "You think it was my fault the marriage crumbled?"

"I'm sure there was plenty of blame to spread around. But Miguel, you knew what the theater meant to her when you married her. You went into it with your eyes open."

"Actually, I didn't. I had no idea what kind of a commitment it was until I was living with her," he countered softly. "It came as a surprise how much of her time and energy went into it. I guess I could have been more patient. But I wasn't." He waved his hand above his head. "And now it's too late."

"Maybe not," *Abuelita* murmured. "Do you regret the divorce?"

He did, but he'd be damned if he'd admit it. "Why do you ask? You never liked Vivienne to begin with."

"No, I didn't. But I like divorce even less. And as far as the church is concerned, you're still married. You've not taken the steps to have it annulled. Why not?" *Abuelita* pressed.

"I don't have to," he replied. "We didn't marry in the Catholic church. I don't need an annulment. If I had married in the Catholic church I would get it annulled. Anyway, this is water under the bridge. It's over between me and Vivienne. I don't want to get back on the Durango Street merry-go-round with her, and the last thing she wants back is a moneygrubbing workaholic. Her words, not mine."

"I see," his grandmother murmured. "And you are quite sure of that."

"Ah-huh."

"Even though you're lonely all the time and working horrible hours to have something to do?" Mama asked softly. When he looked at her in surprise, she said, "A mother knows these things."

"If it comes down to being lonely versus the fights we were having there at the end, I'll take loneliness hands down. Loneliness is nice and quiet."

The two women exchanged a look. "If you say so, *mijo*," his mother murmured.

"Right now, we gotta get through this production. We have to work together without killing one another. I'm not looking forward to it."

He wasn't looking forward to it at all.

That's what he would keep telling himself, anyway.

***

Vivienne stifled a growl of frustration and took a deep breath. "Mr. Halpern, we really need that shipment of plate metal we ordered from you last month. It was scheduled to be here last week at the latest and we're still waiting. What seems to be the problem?"

Joe Halpern of Randall Metals cleared his throat. "We were hit with a bunch of orders all at once. We'll have it on the truck as soon as it rolls off the assembly line."

"That's what you told me last week." Vivienne gritted her teeth. "Look, Mr. Halpern, we have a little metal in reserve, but damned little. We need that shipment on a truck to us tonight."

"I see." She could hear him take a breath. "And how long do you think it will be before you can pay us what you still owe for the last shipment?"

So that was it. Vivienne sighed. "Unfortunately, we're still waiting for the contractor to pay us. I promise you, the minute we get payment from them, you will have your money."

"And the minute we have our money for the last shipment, the current order will be on the truck. Good afternoon, Ms. Heiser."

The connection was broken with an audible click. Vivienne swore out loud, not caring who heard her. Talk about being between a rock and a hard place. Without the plate metal order Halpern was sitting on, they wouldn't be able to make the beams for the refinery tank the construction company was building. She picked up the old-fashioned desk phone and punched Cameron's line. "Cam, do we have enough metal in stock to make the beams without the shipment from Randall's?"

Cameron uttered a sharp curse. "Probably not. Are they being shitty about the money we owe?"

"Visualize the turd emoji dancing across your screen."

"Okay. Call around to the other suppliers and see if they can help us out."

It took her a dozen phone calls, and the better part of the afternoon, but she found a small company out of Alabama that could have the metal there in two days. But it was more than what Randall charged them, requiring Vivienne to suck up her pride and call the bank for another business loan. At first, the loan officer declined, but George Collins, the vice president in charge of commercial loans, an old friend of her father's, overrode the refusal. She cringed when Mr. Collins assured her that he was good with making the loan. "It's for Heiser Steel. A name that means something in this city. I'm not a bit worried. We'll get our money."

Feeling like a fraud, Vivienne thanked him profusely. Her fingers trembled as she hung up the phone. She hoped like hell Mr.

Collins's faith in Heiser Steel wasn't misplaced. She glanced at the time on the computer screen. She needed to get to the theater, but had enough time to make a quick check of her email. Her breath caught in her throat. There was an email from the Hill Country bid. She held her breath and opened the email, her spirits sinking down around her ankles as she read that another company had been awarded the contract.

Shit. They had needed to land that job in a big way. She tried yoga breathing and fought the tears. *Please, please,* she thought as she sat back in her chair and stared at the ceiling. *We need a break. We need a break so badly.*

She looked down at the fat file folder labeled "Durango Street Theatre" that had been delivered that morning from Eloy Solomon's office. She hadn't had a chance to examine the documents in detail, but the summary letter estimated the property's worth at around twenty million. Not that the rundown building was worth all that much, but the property it sat on was prime downtown real estate. The theater wasn't old enough or significant enough to interest the conservation society. It would be bulldozed so a high-rise condo or an office building could be built where it sat.

Vivienne swallowed the bile that rose in her throat. *She had the break she needed so badly. It was sitting right on her desk.*

Her half of twenty million would put Heiser Steel back in the black and give her and Cameron a chance to rebuild the company. It would put them back on their feet. It would give them the opportunity to grow the company the way her father and grandfather should have done. It could make the difference in whether Heiser Steel failed or stayed in business.

It could save their ass, big time.

If she could part with the Durango.

Was Miguel was right? Maybe she needed to let go of the theater for the sake of the company.

Vivienne shook her head. She'd pull a Scarlett O'Hara and would think about it later. Right now, she needed to get to the theater. The casting for *Anything Goes* was being announced tonight, and rehearsals would begin right after.

She threw on her cashmere cardigan, a gift from Miguel the first Christmas they were married, then joined the other drivers fighting for space on the roads and expressways in the chilly winter dusk.

The marquee was off, but the lights were on in the lobby. She sailed in, joining the actors milling around, and the familiar faces of Josh and Rachel, as well as the production manager Miranda Jenks, and the local drama professor, Aubrey Ellis, who was directing the play. Vivienne wasn't overly fond of Aubrey's directing style, finding her heavy-handed. But the woman knew and appreciated musical comedy.

Vivienne gave Miranda a quick one-armed hug. "What are you doing here? You usually don't step in until later."

Miranda rolled her eyes. "It was either come here tonight and see who's doing what or go home to a shit-pile of memories that are going to make me cry or hit the bottle, which my AA sponsor wouldn't appreciate. I'd rather stay here."

"Oh, geez, that's right. I'm sorry. I forgot." January was the anniversary month of the accident that had taken Miranda's only child and led to the dissolution of her marriage.

"Every year I think I'm getting better. And then January rolls around and it all comes back with a vengeance." She shook her head, her graying corkscrew curls bouncing around her face.

"Actually, I think you're doing remarkably well," Vivienne assured her friend. "It's good you decided to come tonight." She gave Miranda another hug and then wandered down to the front of the theater.

The actors who knew they had landed some part in the production sat in the first few rows. Wade and Jessica wandered in and took their seats, and Letti came rushing in at the last minute and slid into a chair on the fifth row. Vivienne sat down by herself a few rows back and settled in, relaxing for the first time since her feet hit the floor this morning. She felt the tension of the day melt away, and an excited buzz of anticipation took its place.

Another production was about to begin.

Rachel stood up in front of the microphone. "I want to thank y'all in advance for all the hard work you're going to be doing to make *Anything Goes* a success. Please remember that every part is important, whether you're in a lead role or dancing in the ensemble."

Letti snorted audibly, earning herself a glare from Rachel.

"And here we go. Vivienne Heiser will be our Reno Sweeney." Vivienne waved her hand to an enthusiastic round of applause.

Rachel smiled and looked down at her sheet. "Wade Baxter will be our Billy Crocker."

Wade smiled to another round of applause. "Recent Academy graduate Hector Delgado will play Moonface Martin. Congratulations, Hector, and welcome to the adult stage." A huge smile bloomed on the young man's face as he stood up and took a bow. "And our Hope Harcourt will be Jessica Clary."

A huge smile bloomed on Jessica's face and she waved her hand at the applause. Letti stiffened in her seat and glared at Rachel and Josh. *Uh-oh, those two are gonna be on her shit list for a while.* No worries. They had broad shoulders and could take Letti's snark. But if Letti said one word to Jessica, Vivienne would personally rip the woman a new one.

The supporting cast was announced. Anyone who wasn't specifically mentioned was automatically part of the ensemble. Which meant that Letti would either have to be in the ensemble or, more likely, work the show as crew chief.

Manuscripts were handed out and the mic was turned over to Aubrey, who shared her vision for the show with the cast. "I want this to be a blast from the past," she explained. Except for the older characters, the cast was mostly in their twenties or, in Vivienne's case, early thirties. "It's an era none of us remember," Aubrey went on. "So I have an assignment for y'all. I challenge you to find and watch at least five movies, preferably musicals, that were made in the thirties or were about the thirties. Josh or Rachel will be emailing you a list of recommendations. Study the costumes. Listen to the dialogue and the songs. Watch the dancing. Things were done differently back then. Get a feel for the difference. Get a feel for the era so we can recreate it here on the stage."

Vivienne had probably watched every movie on Aubrey's list and then some. But she would watch them again and reacquaint herself with the 1930s.

Aubrey talked for a bit longer, and then Josh and Rachel passed out the rehearsal schedule. Rehearsals would begin almost immediately, giving the actors a matter of days to memorize their dialogue and lyrics. The major characters would meet the following Monday in the rehearsal rooms in the small building adjoining the main theater. The rehearsal rooms were old and cramped and stuffed with teaching materials used by the students in the Academy, but they were cheaper to light and heat than the main stage.

The old building also housed the offices, such as they were, and at times those offices were also used for rehearsal, if no more than two or three actors were involved in a scene. Vivienne had spent some of the happiest hours of her life in those rooms.

Josh and Rachel addressed a few housekeeping details and then everyone was dismissed. Vivienne tucked her manuscript under her arm and headed down the aisle, stopping when Jessica and Wade stepped up for hugs. "Good going, Jessica," Vivienne said as she gave the young actress a huge hug. "I knew you had what it takes to play Hope."

Wade looped an arm around Jessica. "She's got even more to be excited about. Aubrey texted her and said she wants Jessica to choreograph the dance numbers for the show."

Jessica's face was shining. "Can you believe it? As picky as Aubrey is, I would have thought she'd want to do the choreography herself."

Vivienne raised a brow. "Or maybe she wants you to do it because she *is* so picky. Ever think of that?"

"Oh, you're too sweet. I've gotta go talk to Aubrey." She scurried off down the aisle.

Vivienne and Wade watched her go. "Congratulations to you, too," Vivienne said as she squeezed Wade's arm.

His smile was lopsided. "Thanks. It'll seem strange, acting opposite Jessica and not Sandra."

"I know. Have you heard from her?"

"She and Noelle called last week. They're doing fine. She sounds really happy." He started to say more but stopped. "You know, I haven't congratulated you, so let me rectify that. I think you'll be a terrific Reno Sweeney."

"Why, thank you, kind sir." She made a mock curtsey. "You want to go grab some supper somewhere?"

"Don't mind if I do."

He took her elbow and they walked up the aisle and into the lobby, where they found a fuming Letti facing off with an exasperated Miranda. "Damn it, Miranda, I should have gotten the Hope Harcourt role. I can sing circles around Jessica, and I have a hell of a lot more experience than she does."

"Letti, darlin', did you ever stop to think that all your experience might be part of the problem?" Miranda drawled. "Good God almighty, Hope Harcourt's supposed to be nineteen or twenty. You may be beautiful, but you're forty years old, and you look it. No, they weren't going to cast an actress that long in the tooth as Hope. It wasn't gonna happen and if you would put on your glasses and look in the mirror you could see why."

Letti recoiled like she'd been slapped. "I'm not forty," she said through clenched teeth.

"If you're not, you're mighty damned close," Miranda shot back. "If you hadn't been such a diva, you could have had either the Evangeline Harcourt part or Erma Latour. But no, you insist on playing the ingénue and what did it get you? You've ended up moving furniture between scenes, because they're not going to cast you in a role you aged out of fifteen years ago."

"That's a shitty thing to say," Letti sputtered angrily. "I'm supposed to play the mother of a grown woman?"

"No, darlin', it's not me being shitty, it's the truth. And in case you've forgotten, you *are* the mother of an almost grown woman. I know you think getting older is about the worst thing that can happen to you, but trust me, it's not. There are things in this life that are a whole lot worse." Miranda turned on her heel and marched out, slamming the lobby door behind her.

Letti watched her go before turning to Wade and Vivienne. "You'd think she could have been at least a little sympathetic. Instead she ripped into me."

"I don't think she's feeling too sympathetic toward anybody. It's January, remember?" Wade said quietly.

"Oh, crap. It is, isn't it?"

"Sophie's about the same age her boy would have been," Vivienne added. "In her eyes, you have everything she doesn't."

Letti had the grace to look abashed. "I guess I do. Okay, then. She gets a pass." She turned on her heel and followed Miranda out.

Vivienne's lips twitched. "That's what I love about this place. The drama's not all on the stage." Wade laughed and they decided on Mexican food at one of the Market Square restaurants.

As the chilly wind hit her face, Vivienne sighed happily. The magic had already kicked in. They hadn't even started rehearsals and she was already pumped about the show. Adrenaline gushed through her nervous system, making everything come alive, turning her black and white world into a kaleidoscope of rainbows. *She couldn't lose this. She couldn't lose the theater.* It brought color and meaning to her life. It gave her a way to share her gifts of song and dance with her hometown. Because of the Durango, she could bring music and joy to the people of San Antonio. That meant everything.

There had to be another way to save Heiser Steel.

Chapter Four

Miguel parked his car in the lot under the expressway and half-walked, half-jogged through the crisp morning air toward the Durango. The sun shone brightly on the almost deserted streets, the light wind cool but not cold on this Sunday morning in February. The lobby lights were off and the theater appeared empty, but a terse email from crew chief Letti Aldrete informed him that the stage door would be unlocked, that he was expected at ten sharp, and that he should plan to stay until ten or so that night. And that he would be expected to do the same every evening this week.

Tech week, also known as Dead Week, was the week when everything had to come together. This coming Friday was opening night. They had today and four more evenings to put it all together: the stage placement, music, costumes, props, wigs, makeup, lights, sound, and everything else that rounded out the show. Everyone involved would be under tremendous pressure to get it right for the upcoming two-month run.

His gut burned, as much from resentment as from the *chile pequin* hot sauce on this morning's tacos. He didn't want any part of this week, or the next eight weeks to come. He could have used today to catch up on the backlog of paperwork that had piled up in the last two weeks. Or, he could have written a half-dozen bids for commercial builds, or spent the afternoon with his favorite realtor scouting for the high-end residential fixer-uppers his company specialized in. Instead, he was stuck here until who knew how late carting crap on and off the stage. "Damn you, Joe Lang," Miguel muttered under his breath. "Couldn't you have paid me back the money and been done with it?"

He took a deep breath and willed himself to calm down. Nothing would be accomplished by being a hardass in front of Vivienne's theater buddies. That would play right into Vivienne's hands.

Nothing would give her and her friends more pleasure than for him to be a dick about having to participate. He'd be damned if he gave them that. He would be pleasant if it killed him. He wondered how Heiser Steel was faring since he'd last spoken to Vivienne and Cameron. He hadn't seen either of them since auditions four weeks ago, but he knew from prior experience that casting was announced a week after auditions and rehearsals started almost immediately after that. The cast had been preparing for a month already. Had Vivienne had taken any time to manage her ailing company, or had *Anything Goes* gotten the bulk of her effort and attention?

Miguel shrugged it off. He had no control over how Vivienne spent her time and energy. He opened the stage door and followed the same path through the back of the theater he'd traveled before, and found a surprisingly small group of unfamiliar faces milling around the foot of the stage. Damn. It was a bunch of kids. Not a one of them was over twenty-five. He was the only one in the whole damn crowd who was in his mid-thirties.

Nope, there were going to be two of them well over thirty, he thought as the woman he recognized as Letti Aldrete came in carrying a clipboard and a copy of the manuscript. Interestingly, she didn't look particularly happy to be here. She had them all sit down, thanked them for agreeing to be on her crew, and explained how they would be spending their day.

And an interesting day it was, Miguel had to admit. Letti took them through the play scene by scene. The stage set of the deck of a New York-to-London ocean liner was already built and in place. It would stay out for the entire performance, lit up when the scene took place on the deck and unlit for the bar and stateroom scenes.

With Letti directing them from a seat in the front row, she determined the placement of each piece of furniture in each scene, as the crew, Miguel included, obligingly moved the pieces this way and that. When she was satisfied, they spiked the set pieces with colored tape and marked the outline of the set piece on the floor. A crewmember or several members were assigned to place the set pieces before the scene and remove them afterward.

When one of the younger crewmembers complained that they could have used a few more people on the crew, Letti explained that she would be using ensemble actors to help with the scene changes, as it cut down on the number of people backstage. The process was long and painstaking, but Miguel found it fascinating despite his antipathy at having to be involved.

It took them the rest of the morning and the entire afternoon to place the furniture and props and spike the pieces. Josh Goldstein came in about five bearing enough pizza to feed an army, and the tired and hungry crew polished off most of it. The sound and lighting crews came in, and under the direction of a woman briefly introducing herself as Miranda, they started experimenting with the stage lights and sound. The actors began drifting in and the energy level in the theater rose as their contagious enthusiasm spread to the tired crew.

The thrumming beat of anticipation had increased exponentially by the time Vivienne strolled in. She was wearing the first genuine smile he'd seen on her face in a long time. Excitement gleamed in her eyes as they traveled over the set and around at her castmates. She gave them a big thumbs-up and ran up the steps to the stage two at a time. She was pumped and raring to go. The way she'd always been the week before a production began.

He'd resented the hell out of it when they were married.

And he resented the hell out of it tonight.

Miguel fought back the bitterness. He couldn't change the past, which brought them to this now. He sat down in the front row for a breather until whatever came next. To his surprise, Letti sank down beside him. She still didn't seem overly enthused, but her expertise had been evident all day, and he took the liberty of telling her so.

She looked at him, surprised. "Why, thank you. Crewing isn't one of the more glamorous contributions to a production, but the actors would be up shit's creek without us. Especially the children."

"What children? There are no children in the cast."

Letti grinned wickedly. "Not this cast. There are three more casts, however, made up of the Academy kids. We're teaching them to crew. You'll be expected to help train some of the kids."

"Wonderful," he said dryly. "I wish somebody had thought to tell me."

"Sorry about that." Letti didn't sound one bit sorry. "It's part of being on the crew. I guess they forgot to tell you."

More likely hadn't told him out of spite. But he wasn't going to say it out loud. "Whatever. I thought they were taught crewing in the Academy."

"They are. But they learn from us, too. And you can't reasonably expect ten-year-olds to move that heavy bar into place."

"Ten-year-olds? You have a cast with ten-year-olds?"

"Sure do. An elementary aged cast, a middle school cast, and a high school cast. The high schoolers do have a crew, but we come in and work with them ahead of time. Jessica and her faculty do an awesome job with them." She smiled proudly. "Wait 'til you see the teen performance. My daughter rocks Reno Sweeney."

An older woman who introduced herself as Aubrey sat down beside Letti, who turned to Miguel and said, "Aubrey's the director. When she sits down here, it's our signal to get back to work."

Miguel and the rest of the already tired crew put in four more busy hours as the cast performed on the stage for the first time. The colored tape came out again as the stairs from the upper to lower decks were Glo-taped so the actors could see them in the dark. Aubrey and the good witch from *The Wizard of Oz* production, who someone finally introduced as Jessica, placed the dancers on stage in position for each dance number. The actors were not in costume yet. They were dressed in a hodge-podge of rehearsal outfits leaving him unsure what role the actor was playing.

But there was no doubt what role Vivienne played. She was dressed in an old baggy T-shirt, leggings that had seen better days, and leg warmers around her ankles, with her hair scraped back and not a lick of makeup. Plain as the day is long, she used to say about her looks. She was wrong, but she never believed him, so he stopped telling her.

The minute she stepped into her role as Reno Sweeney, she *was* Reno Sweeney. She became the brash, beautiful nightclub singer turned evangelist. She oozed Reno's self-confidence and beauty from every pore.

He never had figured out how she, or other actors, transformed themselves before his eyes. They were a different breed, like some type of shape shifter.

The cast went through the play scene by scene, adding in the actors and the lighting to the set changes they'd put together earlier in the day. The musicians were there for the first time, too, ensconced in their sound booth upstairs with their musical director. Miguel knew from his years with Vivienne that tonight was the band's first run-through with the cast, and that earlier rehearsals had been with keyboards only.

A lot of things would be coming together as the week progressed, new elements added each night and rough spots ironed out. By Thursday, dress rehearsal night, everyone involved would be exhausted, hence the cynical but honest description of it as Dead Week. But, at the same time, they would be pumped and ready, eager to strut their stuff on opening night.

It was after ten when they finished going through the last dance number. Miguel found himself impressed by the tap dance numbers Jessica had choreographed. She was doubling as the Hope Harcourt character. He'd seen good dancing over the years at Durango, but these numbers were going to knock the audience out of their seats. He stepped over to congratulate her and realized that he already knew her from some of the cast parties Vivienne had thrown at their condo. "Great dance numbers," he told her.

She smiled shyly. "Thank you. It helps when you have talented dancers like Vivi and Wade."

"And you."

"And me." She blushed prettily and scurried off.

He felt a familiar hand on his shoulder as the haunting aroma of lemons and coconut shampoo tickled his nose. "No hitting on Jessica or anybody else in the cast."

He turned around to find Vivienne giving him the stink eye. "Why, *querida*, you make me think you still care." He grinned wolfishly. "You don't want me anymore, *cara*. You delivered divorce papers to me to prove it. So I believe that gives me the right to hit on anyone I care to."

"Not Jessica," she hissed. "She's vulnerable."

"She looks like a big girl to me. Of course, if you're that worried, you could always go a round with me like we used to."

"Up yours, asshole." She turned her nose in the air and marched off.

He snickered even as he felt himself harden. Damn her. He hadn't been hitting on her little friend. Vivienne was the only woman he longed for, but he was shit-sure he'd never let on.

He made a detour to the men's room and was heading out the door when he heard Vivienne's voice coming from a small office off the lobby. "Damn him, he was hitting on Jessica. She's the last one he has any business flirting with."

He slowed down a bit and grinned. Normally he didn't eavesdrop, but for this, he'd make an exception.

"Doth the lady protest too much?" Josh Goldstein snickered. "Perhaps a bit of love still lingering?"

"Hardly. There was never any love in the first place. On his part or mine. It was a marriage brokered in financial heaven."

"Harsh, Vivi."

"Harsh, but true. I wish to hell Uncle Joe hadn't concocted this harebrained scheme to have Miguel down here. He's the last person we need working a show."

"Oh, but I beg to differ. Maybe if your ex is exposed to what we do, he'll come to appreciate the worth of the theater and won't be so eager to sell the Durango out from under us."

"Miguel appreciate the Durango? That's a laugh. He appreciates the worth of the theater's sale price. He could work every show from now until eternity and he wouldn't care about the theater, the productions, or what we do for the community."

Josh was right. Vivienne's opinion of him was harsh.

"Are you sure of that?"

"Sorry to say, my ex is obsessed with a buck. Even if he thought what we are doing was worthy, he wouldn't let that get in the way of making a profit. He makes all his decisions with the bottom line in mind. Even his choice of bride was made with dollar signs in his eyes. I was merely another asset in his portfolio. C'mon. I'm not exactly the kind of woman a man dreams of having in his bed."

Damned if that's the truth. He dreamed of her in his bed every night.

"He married me to gain entry to San Antonio society. To have access to Tripp Heiser's business connections, and his daughter on his arm at all the society shindigs he couldn't get into himself. Do you honestly think he would have looked twice at me if my dad had been a teacher or a construction foreman?"

"I-I don't know," Josh stammered.

"He married me for what I could do for him," she spat bitterly. "Plain and simple. He didn't give a shit about Vivienne Heiser the woman."

*And you didn't give a shit about Miguel Abonce the man, Vivi.
All you wanted was a meal ticket.*

Not waiting to hear more, Miguel stomped all the way to the parking lot. Shit. Making him sound like he'd used her. Maybe he had, but she'd used him as shamelessly.

He found her Beamer parked next to his Lexus and took out his phone to put its car holder when he saw he'd missed a call from his mother. Alarmed, he called her back and she assured him everything was fine and that she'd called to check in with him. He unlocked his car and was about to get in when Vivienne ran across the street. "Fancy meeting you here," she muttered as she beeped her car open.

"Imagine that. Did you get finished saying shitty things about me to Josh and decide to go home?"

"No. Actually, I could have gone on a lot longer than I did. Too bad you didn't stay a little longer. I really got going after you walked away." Huh. She'd known he was there.

"I heard enough, believe me. But you left out some things, didn't you? Like the fact that you jumped at the chance to marry me to continue to enjoy the lifestyle you couldn't pay for any more."

Vivienne shrugged. "It was the least you could do. Your income doubled the first year we were married, thanks to all the business you picked up from Daddy's old friends."

"Maybe. But you don't have to make it sound like I took advantage of you, because I sure as shit didn't. You got a hell of a lot outta me every damned day of the three years we were married." He stepped closer to her. "And you got something else out of it, didn't you, *güera?* The best sex of your life, you told me repeatedly."

"All that empty, meaningless sex we used to have." She took a step closer to him. "You loved it too." She poked a finger in his chest. "So, *please* don't pull this shit like it was one-sided."

"Yeah, I liked it. Still do, come to think of it." He slid his arms around her. "Let's see if we like it as much as we used to."

Slowly he drew her closer, giving her plenty of time to pull away. But not Vivi. She met him halfway. With no real height difference between them, their lips met straight on as they always had. At first the kiss was tentative. It had been a while. Miguel breathed in the familiar coconut and lemon of her hair as he yanked her against him, toe to tongue. He'd missed that smell, and her soft hair draped on the pillow inches from his nose. She cupped his face between her palms as she deepened the kiss, her tongue snaking into his mouth and ensnaring his in a sensuous duel. She'd kissed him like that often, cradling his face in her hands as she explored his eyes and his nose and his cheeks with butterfly kisses.

He'd missed those kisses when she left him.

His breath hitched in his throat as his cock banged against the zipper of his jeans. He felt her nipples pucker under the loose T-shirt and pictured her naked breasts, high and firm, and oh so responsive to his touch.

He ran his hand down her rounded ass, tight and shapely with the muscles of a dancer, and pictured it poking up in the air, pink from a sexy spanking, waiting for him to shove his cock inside of her warmth.

He tangled his legs with hers and imagined them wrapped tightly around his waist as he thrust himself into her as she cried out and came in his arms. He remembered the way her lips and tongue had closed around his cock, milking him until he gave it up. Damn, he'd hoped the attraction had faded. But, hell, his desire for her was stronger than ever.

He should pull away. Instead, tightened his hold while he plundered her sweetness. They clung together for long moments, their moans the only sound in his ears. When he pulled back, he looked into her eyes, dimly lit by the streetlights and a waxing moon in the night sky. "Well," he murmured softly as he took in her swollen lips and her glazed expression. "Was it as good as it used to be?"

His question seemed to snap her out of her trance. "Yep. Best empty, meaningless kiss I've ever had." Her words were biting, but her expression screamed sad. She pulled back and he let her go, even though every muscle in his body was dying to hold onto her.

She got into the Beamer and in typical Vivienne fashion pulled out of the parking lot a little too fast. He watched her go, his fingers pressed to his lips. It stung more than he cared to admit that she thought what he craved was empty and meaningless.

It had never felt that way to him.

**

Vivienne's body shook while she waited at the red light a few blocks from the turnoff to her quiet, tree-lined street. Her trembling hands gripped the wheel tightly as she fought tears. She shouldn't have kissed Miguel. She couldn't blame him. He'd given her plenty of opportunity to back away, to remove herself from his embrace. Which was what she should have done. Instead she kissed him as passionately as he kissed her and rekindled all the old feelings of desire she should have put aside.

She *had* put them aside—well, as much as possible. Then Joe, damn him, threw them together. And damn if the lust and passion hadn't resurfaced as hot and irresistible as ever.

But it meant nothing. It was lust and hormones. Nothing more. When they were dating and during the early days of their marriage, she'd tried to convince herself sex had meaning. But as their relationship soured, she was forced to face the heartbreaking truth. Without love, affection or respect, even great sex was empty and meaningless. As horny as Miguel made her, she needed more than physical desire and release. She needed the love that Miguel could never give her. And she'd never given him.

She needed to love, and to be loved in return.

She would settle for no less in her next relationship.

The light changed and in a couple of minutes she was pulling into her condo's parking lot. She ran upstairs got into a hot shower, washing off rehearsal sweat—and Miguel's touch. Lips. Scent. *Shit.*

She pulled on silk pajamas and a robe and was rummaging around in her refrigerator when she heard a knock on the front door. She checked the peephole, and then opened the door to her smiling mother, dressed in an expensive yoga outfit and clutching a brochure. "I know it's late, but Katie and I had the most wonderful idea, and I couldn't wait to tell you about it."

Vivienne eyed the brochure suspiciously. "And what would that wonderful idea be?"

Her mother hurried in and thrust the brochure at her. "A privately guided trip to France and Italy. Fifteen days with our own private guide and driver. They'll custom tailor the trip to be anything we want it to be. Oh, Katie's so excited. We tried to book it tonight, but the office is closed. We'll call them in the morning."

Vivienne scanned the brochure and handed it back to her mother. "And where do you plan to get the ten thousand each to pay for this?"

"We'll charge it to the company like we always do."

Vivienne didn't even try to bite back her sigh. "No, you won't charge it to the company, because the company doesn't have twenty thousand to send you two off for an adventure. What part of 'seriously in trouble' can't you and Aunt Katie comprehend?"

"It's not that much," Betsy pouted.

"Mom, I keep telling you that we're having trouble paying our suppliers."

"But we haven't been on a trip in forever." Betsy jerked the brochure out of Vivienne's hand. "If you'd sell the theater like Miguel wants you to, you could get Heiser Steel back in the black and things would be like they used to be. You don't need that damned theater, you or Cameron."

Vivienne walked into the kitchen and brought back her biggest knife. She handed the knife to Betsy and held out her right arm. "Go ahead. Cut it off. I don't need it either."

Betsy's lips tightened. "Fine. You've made your point." She walked in the kitchen and threw the knife on the counter. "No sale. Heiser Steel goes belly up and Katie and I live on our Social Security checks."

"Damn it, Mom, Cameron and I are trying to salvage the mess Daddy and Granddaddy left us. But that theater's everything to me. I'll give it up if I have to, but not unless there is absolutely no other way I can go. And I'll be damned if I sell it so you and Aunt Katie can go through money like there's no effing tomorrow."

"Fine. Forget I said anything," Betsy huffed. She squinted at Vivienne. "If you'd stayed married to Miguel like you should have, it wouldn't be an issue."

"Actually, it probably would. It was never in the blueprint for Miguel to bail out Heiser Steel. Even he's not that rich."

"He could have helped some. And you wouldn't be living in a run-down condo driving a two-year-old car and sporting an inch and a half of brown roots." She shook her head. "You really ought to make it up with him, Vivienne."

"Fine. I'll make an appointment with Claudette. But I am *not* going to get back with Miguel." She sank down on the sofa and put her head in her hands. "I should never have married him in the first place. Biggest mistake of my life."

Betsy sat down across from Vivienne and leaned forward. "Why would you think a thing like that? You were good for one another."

And good with one another, too. But she'd never say that to her mother.

"If you mean his money for my social connections, we were great together. If you're talking about any basis for a real marriage, we didn't have a damned thing going for us."

"I'm afraid you lost me, Vivienne. What do you think your marriage was missing?"

Vivienne looked up at her mother. Betsy was genuinely puzzled. "We didn't love each other. We each went into the marriage for what we could get from each other. When it got shitty, we couldn't hold it together because there was nothing there."

"You didn't try hard enough."

"No, we didn't, because we didn't give a big enough damn about each other. If we'd loved one another even a little, we might have been able to make it work. Like you and Daddy did."

Betsy laughed derisively. "You know better than that. Your father and I married for the same reasons you and Miguel did. He was the fourth-generation scion of Heiser Steel and I came with a society pedigree and a generous trust fund. We liked each other well enough and shared enough common interests that we enjoyed our life together, but our relationship was hardly the stuff of epic love stories. And we weren't the only ones." She laid her hand on Vivienne's arm. "Honey, most of the marriages in our circle are made for financial advantage. Oh, a few of my friends were, or thought they were, madly in love with their husbands. But most of us knew better."

"But that's what I want. To love him and be loved in return."

Her mother's mouth tightened. "Then I'd have to say, good luck with that. There was nothing wrong with my marriage to your father, believe me." She paused a minute. "Maybe you ought to delete all the romances from your Kindle and download a few murder mysteries instead. You wouldn't be entertaining such ridiculous ideas."

Betsy picked up her brochure and left. Vivienne stared at the front door long after her mother shut it behind her. She shouldn't have expected Betsy to understand. Her parents had made a financially advantageous marriage, and they'd had enough in common to make their marriage work. But it wasn't what she wanted for herself anymore. The next time she married, if there was a next time, she would love the man. And he would love her just as much.

There would be no more bargains like the one she'd made with Miguel Abonce, even if his kisses left her on fire.

Too wired to sleep, she made herself a sandwich and sat down at the counter with her laptop. Tomorrow was going to be a long day and it wouldn't hurt to get a head start. She opened the company site and started going through the emails that had come in since Friday afternoon. Ten minutes later she wished she'd left it until morning. Another badly needed bid had been rejected, and three more suppliers had sent nasty-grams about their unpaid accounts.

Between Miguel's kisses, her mother's visit, and the emails, Vivienne's earlier euphoria had evaporated and was replaced by a sinking feeling in her gut.

Again she was forced to face facts. Heiser Steel was in trouble and getting deeper in trouble by the day. Short of a miracle, or the sale of the Durango, the company was going down. Soon she could be faced with the choice of keeping the theater or saving the family business.

Shit.

Chapter Five

Miguel carried his sack of tacos out of the hole-in-the-wall Mexican restaurant and dragged his tired ass to the Durango. The late afternoon sun shone weakly in the west as he headed up the busy sidewalk. He was early, but he had come from a job site south of town and he was too worn out to go to his condo on the north side to shower and change. He had a change of clothes in his duffel and would change in the restroom at the theater.

Letti had given them strict instructions to wear all black and nothing shiny to be as inconspicuous as possible during scene changes, so he'd brought black jeans and a black Henley. He would change and then hide in the balcony with his tacos until it was time for the crew to report in.

They had to sweep the stage, freshen the backstage restrooms, put water in the dressing rooms for the cast, reset set pieces and props, and help the actors get their quick-change costumes ready on racks in the wings. As the actors got into their costumes and head mics, the sound manager would do the sound checks.

Then it would be time for the cast and crew to perform tonight's dress rehearsal. Which better go well. Then, provided there were no fuck-ups or changes needed, they would all go home and then come back tomorrow to do it for real.

Miguel rubbed his eyes. He'd thought after Sunday's marathon he'd been beat. But Monday the actors had added their costumes, performing for the first time in their thirties-style suits and dresses, with Vivienne rocking the signature *Anything Goes* tap-dance in retro wide-legged pants and a sleeveless blouse with wide lapels that plunged deep in the front.

Tuesday they'd added wigs and hairpieces or had their hair done up a la the 1930s. The production manager, Miranda, had made and styled all the wigs and hairpieces. No small undertaking. Last night they had all applied their stage makeup for the first time, with generous advice from Letti, who apparently had more experience than most of the cast with period stage makeup.

Every evening there had been copious notes from the director, the production manager, and the artistic director troubleshooting, tweaking, and making changes that would improve the play. Tonight they would put it all together in the last rehearsal before they opened tomorrow.

Vivienne was always eager and pumped before opening night, but from the tense expressions on Josh and Rachel's faces, not everyone involved was as cheery at the dress rehearsal as his ex-wife. He avoided anyone with a frown on their face and headed up the stairs, where he did the quickest change on record in the mezzanine restroom. He sank down in a balcony chair and was finishing off the last of the tacos when he heard footsteps coming down the aisle. Letti sat down across from him and pulled a wrapped hamburger out of a greasy brown bag. To his surprise, he'd hit it off with the prickly but talented crew chief. "You hiding, too?" she teased as she unwrapped the delicious-smelling burger.

"That would be me." He wadded up the trash and stuffed it in his plastic sack. The curtains were open and Jessica was taking the dancers through one more rehearsal of the big nightclub number at the beginning of Act Two. "Are they as tired as we are?"

"Probably more. Remember, we've been at this less than a week. They've been rehearsing almost since auditions."

"I remember. Vivienne would disappear the minute she landed a role and surface three months later." He cringed at the bitterness in his tone.

"Tell me what you really think." Her dark eyes danced.

He watched the dancers on the stage for a couple of minutes. "Even after being married to Vivienne, I never realized how much work goes into a production until now. Tell me, why do you all put yourselves through this? Every one of you works long hours at a day job, yet you come down here and spend hours and hours putting together a professional-quality show. And you don't get paid a fucking dime."

"Actually, I do get a tiny honorarium. Tiny being the operative word. But you're right. The actors get squat."

He turned to her. "So why, then?"

"Once an actor, always an actor. If it's in your blood it never goes away. Any chance to tread the boards and perform in front of a live audience is an addiction you never lose. After that, everyone's got a different story.

"Me? I'd planned to take Hollywood by storm before I got pregnant with Sophie and married Owen Aldrete. If you ask most of the others, Vivienne especially, they'll tell you that they believe in the need for local artistic productions, both for those who want to participate and those who want to sit back and enjoy. I know Cameron blows out his butt about how she should have gone on to Broadway. And I'm betting she would've done well. But Vivi loves the Durango and believes in what we're doing here. And all of us, Jessica and Josh in particular, are passionate about what they're doing for the kids in the Academy. Have you seen them in action yet?"

"Who? Jessica and Josh?"

"No. The kids. Let me finish this burger and I'll take you next door for a look."

Letti downed the rest of the burger in three bites. His plans to chill undone, Miguel followed her to the building next door, which was a beehive of activity. Parents congregated in the lobby, lounging in folding chairs and chatting with one another. Several greeted Letti with a wave and a smile. He followed her down a narrow hall to a mirrored rehearsal room, where a group of high-school-aged dancers were performing the exact same routine he'd seen on the main stage. Letti gestured toward a beautiful young girl in the middle of the dancers who bore a striking resemblance to her. "That's my Sophie. She's playing Reno Sweeney."

"Beautiful girl. You must be proud."

"I am." They stopped to watch for a couple of minutes. Miguel noticed that one of the girls on the second row of dancers had Down Syndrome, although he wouldn't have guessed it from her dancing.

Letti led him around the edge of the room and into another, smaller room, where a group of much younger girls were "sweeping" the floor and singing "It's the Hard-Knock Life." They probably ranged from five to maybe ten or eleven. They were all shapes, sizes and ethnicities. One of the older girls was missing most of her left forearm. The instructor, a middle-aged woman with a gorgeous smile, was singing along with them, pointing up and down with her finger. They sang the last notes and she shut off an iPhone strapped to her side. "Hello, Miss Letti. To what do we owe the honor of your presence this afternoon?" she asked.

"Just showing Mr. Abonce around. The Academy came up in conversation and I thought he'd enjoy the nickel tour. Miguel, this is Barbara Pierce. She's been teaching with us ever since we opened the Academy."

Miguel shook hands with Barbara. She introduced the little girls one at a time. Most were friendly and smiling, but a couple hung back and had to be coaxed to shake his hand. "Barbara works wonders with the kids," Letti said as they stepped from the room. "She'll have those shy ones out of their shells in no time at all." Letti smiled and winked.

"I'll be damned. I'm impressed. Seriously impressed."

"Good. You should be."

They were walking back into the Durango when his telephone buzzed. He looked down at the number and swallowed. It was a potential buyer for the theater that he'd schmoozed during a Kiwanis breakfast last week. "Excuse me. I've got to take this."

He stepped outside and stood far away from the entrance. "Horace, how can I help you?" he asked.

"I've talked to my partners and we might be interested in purchasing the Durango property. Is there any chance you or your realtor could show us around?"

"The property's not listed yet, but I'd be more than happy to walk you through tomorrow afternoon." They settled on four and Miguel hung up.

Foster headed one of the wealthiest companies in town, and if anyone had the money to buy the Durango, it was Horace. Miguel wandered into the theater and reported to his duty station backstage, wondering why he wasn't more enthusiastic about the visit tomorrow. He should be delighted that a consortium of their stature and wealth was interested in purchasing the property. With their resources, the sale would be quick and sweet, and he and Vivienne would have a hefty profit to split. They could honor Tripp's legacy and save his beloved mentor's company.

Miguel was tempted to call Horace back and cancel. Which made no sense whatsoever.

He was setting up the barstools and tables for the first scene when Vivienne walked in, looking fresh and chipper. "Are we ready to knock 'em dead?" she asked as she danced around the bar.

"I thought that was tomorrow night." He set a stool in front of the bar.

"We'll have a small but important audience tonight. Maggie always invites the local drama critic and someone from the newspaper's events calendar to the dress rehearsals. They usually write an article or a critique for tomorrow's paper. We get a lot of free publicity from them. And there may be others. In some ways, this is opening night." She danced one more pass around the café tables. "Gotta go become Reno."

Every night, he'd marveled at her talent. Vivienne Heiser disappeared and Reno Sweeney took her place. Tonight the transformation would be complete. Reno Sweeney would come alive on that stage.

Miguel's lips lifted in a half smile. "Break a leg, Vivi."

She danced across the stage and disappeared backstage. Miguel watched her, inwardly cursing the persistent longing he felt for her. He'd seen her every evening since their epic kiss in the parking lot Sunday night. And every night he'd gone home to dreams that had him waking up hard as a rock.

Since the divorce, he's dreamed of Vivi on and off, mostly of her coming apart in his arms. But these recent dreams were different. He dreamed of her in the morning, drinking coffee from her favorite mug while she munched on a piece of toast. Or he dreamed of holding hands with her as they meandered down the Riverwalk eating ice cream cones. Last night he'd dreamed of taking her to one of the fancy receptions they'd gone to, her on his arm in all her finery charming everyone at the party. He'd even dreamed of discussing a house renovation with her.

He'd wanted her before, but the attraction had been physical, an itch that a good round of sex would scratch. But now he wanted her for more. He wanted to talk with her, bounce ideas off her, to eat breakfast with her.

Damn. He was screwed.

***

Vivienne whipped into the parking lot across from the theater. She was early, but she'd finished writing up a slew of bids and had emailed them, and it was either sitting in her dreary office hoping for a miracle for Heiser Steel or coming on down to her happy place and chilling a little before it was time to get ready.

Last night's dress rehearsal had gone perfectly, and Jeanine Flores, the local paper's drama critic, had written a delightful review, saying that Vivienne's Reno Sweeney "was as good as Sutton Foster in the recent Broadway revival." Flores had lavished praise on Jessica's choreography, comparing it to that of Hollywood in its golden years.

Josh texted Vivienne and said that due to the favorable write-up, the house was sold out and they'd put in the two more rows of seating in the back that the fire marshal permitted. If tonight's performance went as well as last night's had, and there was no reason why it wouldn't, they had another hit on their hands.

She strode into the lobby, where theater assistant Stanley Herrera was already busy at the concession stand. She smiled and waved and he looked at her a little oddly. Josh and Rachel were standing in the corner, whispering fiercely to one another. They didn't even look up when she walked by. She headed down the theater aisle and up to the stage, where Jessica was working on a dance routine with one of the older teenage boys from the Academy. She looked at Vivienne distractedly. "One of the ensemble called in this morning with the flu. Wesley's stepping in tonight."

Vivienne thanked Wesley, who looked properly nervous. "Anybody else here?" she asked Jessica.

"Just your ex. He's showing some people around."

Vivienne's jaw snapped shut. "Showing *who* around?"

Jessica looked uncomfortable. "Some rich-looking suits. I saw them in the balcony a couple of minutes ago."

"Shit." Vivienne hopped down off the stage and practically ran up the aisle. *The bastard. The sneaky, greedy bastard. Showing the theater to potential buyers on opening night.*

She stopped at the doors to the lobby, breathing deeply and trying to compose herself. The last thing she wanted was to embarrass herself by having a temper tantrum in front of whomever Miguel had with him. It would do her company no good if word got around that the co-owner of Heiser Steel was prone to unwarranted outbursts. She had barely gotten control of herself when Miguel, accompanied by Horace Foster and a couple of Horace's lackeys, came down the balcony stairs. She ignored Miguel entirely and in a manner that would have made her mother proud, straightened her shoulders and approached Horace with a smile on her face. "How are you, Horace?" she asked as she offered her hand.

"Why, Vivienne, what a nice surprise." Horace pumped her hand enthusiastically and looked her up and down. Thankfully, she was still in her clothes from the office and not in her costume and makeup. It would be much easier to make her point looking like a businesswoman. "Miguel tells me you're starring in tonight's opening."

She made her smile brighter. "I certainly am. Right now I'm here as co-owner of the theater."

"Co-owner?" Horace looked puzzled before his face cleared. "That's right. Mr. Abonce did say something about your partial ownership."

"More than partial, Mr. Foster. The theater was left to us jointly. You can't imagine the thrill I feel that Uncle Joe trusted me with his beloved Durango. He loved our productions here, and you cannot imagine the honor of being chosen to see that those productions continue to entertain the people of San Antonio."

Horace's smile faded. "I'm sorry. I don't understand. I thought the Durango property was going on the market soon."

"Certainly not any time in the near future. If I have my way, never."

Horace turned steely eyes on Miguel. "Then what was this afternoon all about?"

Miguel lifted his chin and looked Horace in the eye. "I'm afraid Ms. Heiser and I are having a difference of opinion. I am quite sure she will be coming around to my way of thinking soon."

"That isn't likely to happen." She laid her hand on Horace's arm. "Please don't count on it. If you're looking to make an investment soon, you would do so much better to look elsewhere than to wait for me to change my mind. I'm so sorry Miguel wasted your afternoon."

"So am I." He graced Miguel with a blistering glare. "Call me if and when you and Ms. Heiser come to some sort of consensus."

Horace and his lackeys swept from the lobby. She waited until the doors closed behind the Foster entourage then rounded on

Miguel. But he beat her to the punch. "Why the hell did you run him off?" Miguel snarled. "You made me look like an idiot."

"You *are* an idiot. Bringing in somebody to look at the place behind my back, knowing I'm not selling. Which is why in the hell I ran him off. How *dare* you? What makes you think you have the right to bring some asshole potential buyer through here on *opening night*, trying to sell the theater out from under us?"

"I have every right. I own half the place and I have every damned right to parade them down the aisle five minutes before curtain if I feel like it. Get your head out of the clouds, Vivienne. The fucking theater's going away after this damned farce is over and you and your theater pals need to get used to it."

"You don't own the theater yet and you don't have the right to parade people through here trying to sell it. And you won't ever have that right. Not if I don't sign those papers, asshole. I'll *never* sign. You can take it to the bank. Damn you, Miguel. We've worked our butts off for weeks and you bring those assholes in two hours before curtain and ruin everything for us." Vivienne cursed the tears that spilled out of her eyes. "You're a fucktard." She pulled her bag tight against her. She needed to hang onto something.

Cursing the tears falling on her cheeks, she ran from the lobby to the women's dressing room. *How could he?* As hard as they'd worked, how could he show it to buyers on opening night? As much as it pained her, she knew she might have to sell. But did he have to rub it in her face, tonight of all nights? How greedy and hard-hearted could he be?

She let herself cry for a couple of minutes before taking a breath and composing herself. She wouldn't let him get to her. She wouldn't let the asshat win. He wasn't worth it. Vivienne blew her nose and treated her eyes to a generous helping of eye drops. She went into the bathroom and ran ice water on a washcloth, then returned to the dressing room and sat with her head back, the washcloth over her face. After a few minutes, she straightened, tossed the washcloth on the counter then changed out of her office clothes. She draped a cape around her shoulders then, using stage makeup, she began to apply the thirties-style "face" Reno Sweeney would have put on, but with more color and broader strokes.

Miguel wasn't going to win this round.

Reno was coming in all her glory.

And she was going to kick his ass.

***

Miguel watched with narrowed eyes as Vivienne raced down the aisle and up the stage steps. *Damn it to hell.* She'd made him look like a *pendejo* in front of one of the most influential businessmen in town. She knew as well as he did that they had to sell the theater if she and her brother were going to keep their fucking company. Which made Miguel even madder. Here he was, trying his damnedest to save her family's company, and she was fighting him every step of the way.

His face burned as he realized he and Vivienne had had an audience and that Josh, Cameron and Jessica were all gathered with Stanley and Rachel by the concession stand. None of them looked happy.

He started into the theater but Jessica jumped in front of him, her finger pointed in his face. "You son of a bitch," she ground out. "Pulling a stunt like that two fucking hours before she has to go on. What kind of a greedy SOB are you?"

Miguel gulped. Sweet and gentle Jessica Clary was the last person he would have expected to deal out a public ass chewing. "He asked to see the property and I showed it to him. No big deal," he answered through stiff lips.

"No big deal?" Jessica's face reddened. "You parade rich buyers through the place on opening night trying to sell it out from under her after she's worked for weeks to get a show ready and you don't think it's any big deal? You know how she feels about this place. How could you do that to her?

"I'd like to know how he can do it to any of us," Josh stated. He came to stand next to Jessica. "You know how hard we've all worked to put this show together. Hell, you were part of it. And then to turn around and do something like that."

"Really shitty. Big time," Rachel added.

"I'm not doing anything to you." Miguel looked at all of them with contempt. "Your idealistic friend and her equally delusional brother think they are going to pull a rabbit out of a hat and save the company that's been in their family for five fucking generations that they are within weeks of losing. They refuse to face the fact that the only way they can save that business is to sell the theater. So no, I don't give a damn about the Durango Street Theatre. Or your precious productions." He ignored their gasps. "I do care about the business my friend and mentor left to his children. And I intend to save it. With his children's cooperation or without it."

"Keep telling yourself that, asshole." Cameron looked at him with scorn. "You couldn't care less about Heiser Steel. You want the ten million that you'll earn from your half of the sale."

Miguel felt his face flush even deeper. "That's bullshit." He took a step closer to Cameron. "You know better than that. I loved Tripp, and I'm going to save his business." Miguel wanted to punch Cameron. "You don't give a shit about the company and it's your damned legacy. Maybe you ought to put on your big-boy boxers and persuade your sister to do the right thing." He looked around. "Understand now?"

"All too well," Josh snapped. He turned and walked off.

"Amen to that," Jessica said. "Sorry, Miguel. Cameron's right. It's your half of the money that's calling your name." She headed up the theater aisle.

Rachel curled her lip. "Like you need any more money." She tossed her head and marched away.

Cameron shook his head. "No wonder she was relieved when the divorce was finalized." Then he turned on his heel and left.

That they thought him so crass and greedy stung, but Cameron's parting shot hurt.

Miguel ignored the cold shoulder he was getting from the cast and crew as word of the altercation spread. As he worked through his pre-performance responsibilities, he realized he'd been tactless this afternoon. He could have waited until next week to take Horace on the grand tour. He could have let them have their opening night. They had worked their asses off, and if they turned in less than a stellar performance tonight, it would be his fault.

Chapter Six

Vivienne sat patiently on a stool in the crowded dressing room watching as the other actors did their faces and hair, then put on their head mics and struggled into their costumes for tonight's performance.

Jessica stood behind Vivienne and parted her hair as Miranda had taught them. With a miniscule spring, Jessica secured the tiny lavalier microphone right at the hairline on Vivienne's forehead. Her friend ran the mic wire down the part, securing it every couple of inches until it emerged from her nape, at which point she taped it down to run into Vivienne's costumes. The body pack would be concealed as far as possible beneath the costumes, and would, for the most part, be inconspicuous.

Most of the actors wore headset mics, with a tiny mic inches from the actor's lips, but the Durango had used some of the money from last year's gala to buy the more sophisticated hairline and forehead mics for their production leads to use. If the upcoming gala was equally successful, Josh and Cameron were already planning to invest in more of them.

If there was another gala. The theater might well be history before the next gala rolled around.

Vivienne steered her thoughts in another direction. Now was not the time to think about what ifs. Letti had called the twenty-five-minute mark until the curtain swept open on the first scene. Vivienne sat obediently until Jessica taped the wire down her back and secured the body pack in the waist of the tight pantyhose Vivienne would wear for the entire show. She swept her hair in a flat bun on top of her head and settled Reno's elaborate hairpiece, pinning it tightly and blending it seamlessly with her own.

She checked her makeup one more time and slipped into the over-the-top cocktail dress she wore in the first scene. She would have to make multiple costume changes during the show, in a couple seconds while standing in the wings, stripping down in front of everyone backstage. It didn't bother most actors, her included, to be seen virtually naked by the cast and crew, but it had always bugged the hell out of Miguel. Vivienne smiled to herself. His lips had tightened during her first quick change during dress rehearsal, but he'd seemed unconcerned through the rest of the production.

She hoped it bugged him again tonight. It would be a petty revenge after what he'd done to her and the cast earlier this afternoon, but she wasn't above dealing out whatever misery she could cause him. Without speaking a word, the cast and crew let him know what they thought about this afternoon's stunt. Not that the bastard cared. All he could see was a check for ten million dollars with his name on it.

Shit. She was thinking about him again instead of concentrating on the performance. Jessica sat down on the stool Vivienne had vacated and she repeated the hairline mic process on Jessica, who had already given Vivienne a blow-by-blow of the ass-chewing she and the others had treated Miguel to. "Not that it seemed to get through to him," she'd complained. "He's a cold one, your ex."

They got Jessica's mic in place and concealed under her thick blonde hair, perfect for ingénue Hope Harcourt. They were securing the body pack when Letti poked her head in the door. "Are you all right?" she asked Vivienne. "Rachel's concerned that you're upset and your performance will suffer. I tried to tell her you're more professional than that but she's still worried."

Vivienne bit back annoyance. "Tell Rachel I'm fine." She looked around at the women in the crowded dressing room. They were all listening avidly. "In fact, I'm more than fine. And so is everybody else. We're gonna rock tonight. We're gonna put on the show of a lifetime. How 'bout it, ladies?"

The dressing room erupted in applause. Letti gave them a thumbs-up. "I'll let Rachel know." She grinned devilishly. "And I'll make sure the guys get your message. We'll show our favorite jackass what the Durango is capable of."

For the second time that day, tears threatened. "Thanks, all of you." Vivienne sniffed them back and smiled. "So let's all break a leg."

Jessica hustled into her costume. They did a last-minute costume and makeup check, and then Vivienne took her place in the wings, brushing past Miguel without so much as a glance. Wade took his place beside her and gave her a squeeze. "I hear we're putting on the performance of a lifetime tonight," he murmured loudly enough for Miguel to overhear.

She smiled up at him. "That we are."

"Good. Let's give the audience their money's worth."

And they did. Spurred by their ire, the cast put on a performance that could only be described as incredible. Vivienne felt herself bring Reno to life, channeling her anger into an over-the-top performance she didn't even know she was capable of. Every note, every dance step, and every perfectly delivered line said she was Reno. And Reno kicked ass. Wade and Jessica were over the top wonderful, and Hector knocked it out of the ballpark. The supporting and featured cast all handed in stellar performances. Even the ensemble rocked.

And not a one of them looked at Miguel.

Vivienne's good mood was more than restored, and the cast basked in the claps and whistles and stomps of a long, enthusiastic standing ovation. The patrons were gushing their delight as they shook hands, hugged their favorite actors and got them to pose for pictures.

The cast milled around obligingly until the last of their audience had bid them a good evening, and then, as the euphoria faded, they trudged back to the dressing room to change into street clothes. Jessica and Vivienne removed each other's mics and, gratefully, Vivi stripped out of the last costume of the evening so the body pack could come off. She looked at the office outfit she'd worn earlier and made a face. "I should have brought something else to throw on to drive home."

"Why bother? You're going to take them off the minute you get home." Jessica's phone beeped and she looked at the screen. "Uh-oh. Bobby's been busy." She laughed and showed Vivienne the screen. Jessica's young son had sprayed himself with whipped cream from his neck to his waist.

Vivienne laughed. "I bet your mom's fit to be tied."

"Don't kid yourself. She and Daddy love every minute with him."

Vivienne took one more look at the child's picture, hoping her wistfulness didn't show. She and Miguel had never discussed having babies. Admittedly, it had made the divorce easier and less messy with no children involved. But at thirty-three she worried she'd run out of time. If she was going to have a family, it would have to be soon. Unbidden, a vision of a small, dark-haired child with Miguel's strong, even features danced through her mind. No way. If she ever had a child, it wouldn't be Miguel's.

***

Exhaustion hit her as Vivienne pulled into the condo parking lot. She dragged herself up the stairs and into the tiny living room, where she stripped out of her clothes and left them piled on the sofa. She treated herself to a long, hot shower and was crawling into her favorite flannel pajamas when someone knocked on the door.

"Crap," Vivienne snapped as she pulled on a ratty robe. If it was Betsy wanting something else expensive, she was going to get an earful. But it wasn't her mother Vivi spied when she looked out the peephole. Miguel was standing under the porch light with his hands in his pockets.

What the hell?

She turned on her heel and headed toward the kitchen. She'd seen enough of Miguel Abonce today to last her to the next millennium.

He rang the doorbell again, and a third time. Damn it. He'd never been any good at taking no for an answer. If she didn't answer, he wasn't above banging on the door and making a scene. Or worse— getting a key from her mother.

She jerked open the door and glared at him. "What the hell do you want? Haven't you done enough damage today?"

He had the grace to look abashed. "Can I come in? We need to talk."

"I can't imagine what about. You pretty well said it all this afternoon."

"You know damned well what we need to talk about. And we haven't said it all. Not by a long shot." He looked at her with hooded eyes. "Please, Vivi. We have to work together on the show for the next eight weeks. We need to clear the air."

"Whatever." She let him in and shut the door, wondering briefly if she needed to change into something less scruffy, but deciding against it. He'd seen her looking worse than this, albeit not often.

She pointed toward the living room. "Say your piece and go home. I'm tired."

"I can imagine." He moved her pile of clothes to the coffee table and sat down. She sat in the matching chair. "Nice place you have here."

"It's a dump compared to yours and you know it. I meant what I said, Miguel. I'm tired and in no mood to listen to you defend what you did this afternoon. I've told you that as far as I'm concerned, the theater's not for sale. And no amount of bullying or presumptive closes like you tried this afternoon is going to change that."

"Actually, I came by to apologize. It was thoughtless to have them there today. You and the rest of the cast and crew didn't deserve that. Not after all the work you put in."

Vivienne nodded her head once. "Thank you for that." She stared across the room at him, not sure what else to say.

He stared back at her. She could almost hear the gears turning in his head. "Are we going to talk about it tonight? Or wait until later?"

She didn't pretend to misunderstand. "You're here. I'm here. I won't be able to sleep anyway. You may as well go ahead."

He paused as he always had when collecting his thoughts. "I'm not gonna lie to you. Of course, I want my half of the money. It's not quite what Joe owed me, but it would go a long way to cover it."

Vivienne whistled under her breath. "How much did you lend him?"

"Almost fifteen million. Tripp said Joe would be good for it. He was wrong."

"Daddy was wrong about a lot of things," Vivienne said derisively.

Miguel's eyes narrowed. "He was right about a lot of things, too."

"Not about his company, especially the last few years. He left us a mess. Jessica said you threw Daddy in Cameron's face this afternoon. We're pissed off at him with good reason." She rubbed her forehead. "Your relationship with Daddy was much less complicated than ours. You saw him as a valued friend and mentor. A father figure up on a pedestal. Cam and I saw the man who ran through a family's fortune trying to save a company from his bad decisions who left us to pick up the pieces."

"He also left you a business that with an influx of capital could once again be one of the leading companies in this city. You can't let that slip through your fingers, Vivi. Not when you have the means to save it. None of your artsy-fartsy friends believed me this afternoon, but I meant what I said. I *am* thinking about you and yours." He shook his head. "When Joe told me back in November what he'd done, I promised myself I would save Heiser Steel. Tripp did a lot for me and I owe him. And, frankly, you and Cameron don't appreciate what you have. You have no idea what you'll be losing if Heiser Steel goes under."

"Oh, bullshit, Miguel. We know all too well. We grew up listening to Daddy and Granddaddy talk about it over dinner every night. Cameron was on the factory floor by the time he was fourteen. They had me in the office before I could drive a car to get there. They spent money they probably didn't have to send Cam to Wharton School of Business and me to the business program at Stanford. We lived and breathed Heiser Steel, and we were groomed from the nursery to take over someday. We have a damned good grasp of what losing Heiser Steel would mean." She paused. "But do you have any idea what will be lost if the Durango is sold? How much would be lost if the theater closes?"

Miguel shrugged. "Not really. But I guess you're about to tell me."

"There's the obvious. The actors and crew would lose a place to perform. There aren't that many theaters in San Antonio and most of the others are equity or trying to become equity. Which knocks out all the talented amateurs like me who have no desire to go pro."

"It might be a better use of their time and talent if they did go pro."

"Sure. For the two or three who could. The rest, myself included, will be left up shit creek without a paddle." She took a breath. "The Academy would go away. Six hundred children a year go through there. That would be lost. Letti said you were impressed when she took you through and showed you what they are accomplishing. Now think about that being gone."

"Aren't there other programs they could go to?"

"None of our caliber. Six hundred kids, Miguel. Think about it." She sat up straighter. "Now let's talk about how the community will be hurt."

"The community? Isn't that taking this loss thing a little too far?"

"Not at all. The Durango is a San Antonio treasure. We do some of the best shows Broadway has to offer, and we do them well. According to one of the Austin theater critics who comes down to see us, we're better than a lot of stuff being produced off Broadway, and on the California stages. And we do it for a fraction of what the touring Broadway shows cost. Hell, those tickets cost a fortune. Ours aren't much more than a movie. Families who couldn't touch the tickets downtown can come see our shows as often as they'd like. And Josh makes it a point to bring in kids from schools all over town. We're the only live theater they're ever exposed to."

"I've never denied the quality of the productions, or that the Durango is doing good things. You know that."

"But in the grand scheme of things you don't think they're all that important."

"I didn't say that."

"You don't have to. You were honest with me so I'm going to be honest with you. Not acting any more at the Durango would be like cutting off my right arm. I can live without it, but it would be a hell of a loss. But if the Durango is gone the overall loss would be irreplaceable. The adult actors will lose out. The Academy kids will lose out, and all the people who come see us perform will lose out. San Antonio will lose out. So I'm torn. No, I don't want to lose Heiser Steel. But I don't want to lose the theater either."

"I never thought of it that way. It was the hole where you disappeared all the time."

Vivienne winced. "I guess it seemed that way."

"I was jealous."

"For what it's worth, in retrospect I know I neglected you. I am sorry about that."

"I neglected you, too." He shrugged. "Water under the bridge."

She nodded. "Cameron and I will find a way to save the business. I'll be damned if I know how, but we will."

"And if you haven't found a way by the end of the production run? What then?"

"I'll cross that bridge when and if we come to it."

"Whatever." He leaned back and linked his hands behind his head. "I gather the stellar performance tonight was in my honor."

"You could say that. Maybe you ought to piss us off every night."

"Nah. I can do without the deep freeze. That bunch gets any madder at me and the hate stares will burn down the theater." He gave her a sexy grin and Vivienne felt a stab of lust. It was the same provocative grin he'd graced her with the first time they met. She felt her lips curve into a sultry smile.

"Couldn't have that, now could we? Tomorrow night everything will be copacetic and we will be back down to our usual standard of excellence." Her stomach growled audibly. "Crap. I was so pissed off I forgot to eat supper. I need a sandwich. You want one?"

"Sure. I never made my taco run."

Vivienne went into the kitchen with Miguel on her heels. He poked his head in the fridge and smiled. "Ahh, a stocked refrigerator." He started pulling out sliced deli meat and cheese. "Mine's mostly empty these days."

She bit down on a snarky reply and got out sandwich bread and a couple of plates. "Now that it's only me, I usually make a sandwich if I'm home. Or sometimes I bum a meal off Mom and Aunt Katie."

"How's your mother these days?"

"As delusional as ever. She can't or won't adjust to living on a limited amount of money. She and Aunt Katie keep dreaming up expensive crap they want and make me out to be the bad guy when I tell them we can't afford it." She spread mayo on the bread and added the ham and cheese. "This calls for lettuce." She found a head of lettuce in the crisper.

Miguel laid several slices of roast beef on his sandwich. "Give me a leaf or two if you don't mind."

She pulled off a little lettuce for herself and handed him the rest of the head. "How's your mom and grandmother?"

"*Abuelita* hates taking her diabetes shots and bitches about the new neighborhood. Mama makes her take the shots and thinks the new place is heaven."

"Figures." She found two bottles of beer, and they sat side by side at the breakfast bar. They were mostly silent as they wolfed down their sandwiches, and Miguel made himself another.

They'd always been comfortable in silence, until the silences became angry. Tonight the silence was mostly comfortable. But at the same time, Vivienne was oh-so aware of the man sitting next to her. His broad shoulders stretched the material of his long-sleeved shirt. His muscular chest pressed against the fabric every time he moved. And the way his thick, straight hair laid across his forehead, and the sensual curve of his lips, made heat pool at her core.

She'd seen the warmth in his eyes when he'd take her in his arms last week, and she had delighted in the way their bodies fit together perfectly. She couldn't help but wonder if he was as aware of her as she was of him.

She finished her sandwich and looked at Miguel. He took a huge bite out of the second sandwich and looked at her with a gaze that smoldered. "I'm still hungry," he said softly.

Miguel didn't want another sandwich. And they both knew it.

Vivienne sucked in a breath as she stared into his eyes. Ah-huh. The flame still burned for him, too. Her nipples tightened and her breath hitched in her throat. She wanted him as much as she ever had. Even with all that had gone wrong between them, she still wanted him in her bed.

Foolish in the extreme, but there it was.

She reached out and ran her hand down his face. "Do we really want to go there again? After all the shit that's flown?"

Miguel swallowed. "That part was never shit." He reached for her and drew her nearer, until she stood between his thighs. "Even when everything else was going to hell, we could always connect on this level." He tilted her face and pressed his lips to hers.

She told herself to pull away, to take a step back, but his lips touched hers and she was gone. He held her gently at first, but as their passion started to flare, his caress became firmer and more possessive, pulling her into his body as if he owned her. She felt the power of their connection, that steel-strong band of desire that held the two of them in its grip. They'd always felt it, from the moment they'd laid eyes on one another in the tacky little restaurant next door to Heiser Steel.

Craving him in a way she could never explain, she wanted him buried deep in her body, thrusting into her, making her fall apart in his arms. It had been a long drought since she walked out of his door. A drought they were going to break tonight.

No matter how stupid it was.

She looped her arms around his neck as they continued to kiss. For all the passion they'd felt, they had never hurried their lovemaking, always taking their time, savoring every taste, stroke and nibble, letting their desire build until they couldn't take it anymore.

Their caresses were leisurely as they reacquainted themselves with one another's bodies. She stroked his muscled shoulders. He caressed her waist. She ran her fingers through his thick, dark hair. His fingers found one of her nipples and he teased it into a stiff little peak. He tugged her hair, baring her throat as he licked, kissed, and nibbled at the column.

As he lowered her head, he gestured toward the narrow staircase. "Walk or ride?"

She smiled. He'd had a thing about carrying her in his arms. But she couldn't tonight. "Walk."

She took him by the hand and together they climbed the narrow stairs to the second story, past the small second bedroom she used as a home office, then into the larger bedroom furnished with a queen-sized brass bed and an antique cherry-wood dresser and washstand that had been in a guest room in her childhood home.

Miguel's eyes flickered over the elegant old furniture and the handmade quilt on her bed. It wasn't anything like the sleek modern furnishings or satin bedding in the bedroom they'd shared—which was probably why she chose it. She hadn't wanted any reminders of the intimate space she'd lived in with him.

But now she'd have memories of him in this bedroom, too.

Miguel sat down on the bed and kicked off his black sneakers. She let go of his hand and pulled back the covers, exposing simple flannel sheets. She started to untie her robe but Miguel took the sash from her hands and said, "Allow me."

He untied the sash and pushed the robe off her shoulders, kissing the exposed skin of her neck. The pajama top went next. He eyed the faded garment doubtfully. "You don't wear sexy pajama sets anymore?"

She shrugged. "Nobody to wear them for. You still wear black silk boxers?"

He pulled down his jeans, exposing boxer briefs. "Nobody to wear them for."

When they'd met, he'd told her he didn't sleep around, which she'd found surprising given his swagger and good looks. She'd learned his business took up so much of his time and energy that he had little of either to devote to dating and seduction. From the look of the boxer briefs, that was still true.

She didn't know for sure, but she'd bet that there hadn't been anyone in his bed since she'd vacated it. Not because he was still pining over her, or because of a rigid moral code, but because he hadn't taken the time to find anyone else to share it with. Typical Miguel. All business, all the time.

A boon for her. He was probably good and horny by now. She sure as hell was.

With practiced hands they shed each other of their clothing one piece at a time. She pulled Miguel's shirt up and over his head, revealing the hard, muscled chest dusted with the lightest sprinkling of hair and a huge tattoo of an eagle over his heart. More tattoos ran down his arms, intricate designs dating back to his younger days in the barrio.

Broad shoulders and powerful arms spoke to the fact that he wasn't above pitching in on a job site and lifting wood planks and steel bars and heavy chainsaws. Her eyes traveled down to where his treasure trail disappeared beneath the boxers. She hooked her thumbs into the briefs and tugged, exposing his swollen cock jutting up from a nest of dark hair above powerful thighs. A bit more tugging and his jeans and boxers were gone, leaving him naked to her gaze.

Miguel looked at her with a raised eyebrow. "You're overdressed." He pulled down the flannel pajama pants, exposing her to his avid perusal. His gaze traveled her length, starting with her head and neck and then downward, lingering on her breasts and hips. He gazed at the V at the juncture of her thighs, where a patch of light brown hair hid her core. "Beautiful. A dancer's body." He reached out and cupped her hips before running his hands down her legs. "You have the most wonderful legs in the world. I loved when you'd wrap them around me."

"We can arrange for that to happen again tonight."

Miguel's eyes smoldered. He sat down on the edge of the bed and pulled her to stand between his legs, putting his face right at breast level. He teased a nipple with his tongue before taking it in his mouth and sucking, sending shock waves down her body. He knew what she liked. He tormented one breast and then the other, until she was squirming beneath his touch. She wrapped her fingers around his hard, erect cock. It never ceased to amaze her that no matter how many times she touched him, it was always a thrill.

Miguel pushed himself further back on the mattress and pulled her down beside him. Slowly, as though they had all the time in the world, he nipped and nibbled her lips before pushing her onto her back and leaning over her. "Damn, I've missed this," he admitted as his lips traveled down her body, finding and again torturing her breasts into stiff peaks.

Delighted anticipation thrummed through her as he explored her ribs and her lower abdomen. He'd never been shy about going down on her. If anything, he seemed to get a kick out of it, knowing he could make her come apart so easily with his lips and his tongue. He reached the juncture of her thighs and pushed her legs apart, his touch bringing her off the bed. *"Cálmate, mujer,"* he murmured as he settled between her legs. "Lie back and let it roll over you."

After all this time, easier said than done. She snuggled into the sheets, and tried to let the delicious sensations wash over her. Miguel kissed her inner thighs before again caressing her sensitive nub with the tip of his tongue. Christ, he was good at this. She tightened in anticipation, the tension becoming more and more unbearable until it broke, and then powerful tremors coursed through her body to the tips of her fingers and toes.

A lot of men would have taken her orgasm as a signal for him to get his, but Miguel wasn't most lovers. He gave her a moment to catch her breath and then he was at her again, expertly bringing her to a second trembling climax that had her calling out his name. Only then did he move out from between her legs.

"Do we need a condom?" he murmured.

"Only if you…"

He shook his head, and entered her quickly with a single thrust, her drenched core welcoming him. He paused to lean down and took her mouth in a long, lingering kiss. "God, I've missed this."

"So have I."

They moved together as if time hadn't passed. Vivienne wrapped her legs around his hips as he thrust himself inside her, hard and fast. She felt herself spinning out of control, as the two of them climbed higher and higher, until she climaxed once again, crying out his name as she exploded in his arms.

Spurred on by her climax, he too toppled over the edge, calling out her name hoarsely as his body emptied itself into hers. He held on tight as they trembled and shuddered, coming down off a high she'd missed more than she cared to admit.

Without pulling away, Miguel rolled so that they faced one another. A faint sheen of sweat covered his forehead. He ran his fingers down the side of her face. "Fucking awesome."

"It was always awesome," she reminded him quietly. She caressed his powerful chest. "Even when the rest of it was going to shit. I missed it."

"So did I." He grinned devilishly. "I didn't realize how much until now." She felt him start to harden in her body.

"I missed other things, too." She reached down and caressed his balls. "I miss playing ice cream cone with your cock." She raised her brow.

"Actually, my cock seems to be right where it wants to be."

"Jeez, you are getting hard again. Already? I'm impressed."

"It's been over a year, Vivi. I was horny. As fast as you reeled off those orgasms, you're as damned horny as I am."

"So what's with all the blah, blah?" She rolled him and straddled his body. "How many do you think you're good for tonight, Mico?"

He laughed. "Let's go for a record."

Chapter Seven

Vivienne snuggled into the covers, not wanting to wake up. Not wanting to leave the delicious dream of her body entwined with Miguel's while he pounded into her and called out her name. She shut her eyes, hoping she would fall back to sleep and the dream would come back. But from the light filtering through the blinds, she could tell that the sun had been up for at least a couple of hours, and that more sleep wasn't likely. Still, she could shut her eyes again and savor a few more minutes before she had to face the world.

She tried to turn over, but a long arm draped across her waist held her in place. She froze. She was still dreaming. Had to be. She reached down and touched the warm, muscled forearm around her waist. Holy shit. He really was in her bed, and that was his breath dancing softly against her nape. It hadn't been a dream. It had been a memory.

She and Miguel had spent most of the night burning off a year's worth of sexual frustration.

Good God, what had they been thinking? The last thing either of them needed was to complicate what was left of their—relationship.

Even if it had been mighty damned wonderful.

Vivienne stifled a groan and eased out from under his arm, hoping he would sleep long enough for her to gather her thoughts.

She didn't have a clue what to say to him. They'd come to no consensus about the theater. They'd made sandwiches and then they'd fallen into bed, never having finished their discussion about the Durango.

She tiptoed from the room, found jeans and a T-shirt in a pile of clean laundry, and went to the bathroom down the hall. After she cleaned up, she went downstairs and made a cup of coffee. Perched on a barstool, she tried to think of what the hell to say to Miguel, when a key rattled in the lock and Betsy came sailing in with a delicious-smelling paper bag. "Good morning, dear. I thought you'd still be asleep. I was going to leave this on the counter for you. Katie and I went out to that little bagel place for breakfast and we thought you'd like some."

Vivienne's mind raced as she stared at her mother. God only knew what kind of spin she would put on Miguel's presence. Vivienne started to hustle Betsy out the door but could hear Miguel stirring upstairs. He'd be down in no time. She sighed. To hell with it. She'd have to brave it out.

"Uh, thanks." She took the bag from her mother and peeked inside. "Good. There's enough for two."

Betsy's eyes widened. "You're not alone?"

"No, ma'am." Miguel ambled down the stairs, yawning. He'd put on last night's jeans, but his chest and feet were bare. He took the bag from Vivienne and fished out a bagel. "Thanks, Betsy." He took a big bite out of the bagel. "Damn, that's good."

Betsy looked from one to the other, first in shock, but then a slight smile curved her lips. "Sorry. I didn't see your car in the parking lot."

"I changed cars after the divorce."

"That's good. I keep trying to get Vivienne to trade hers in for something newer, but she refuses. Maybe now that you're getting back together, she can get a later model."

"Mom, we're not getting back together," Vivienne said quickly.

"You're not?" Betsy's face fell. She turned to Miguel. "Then what are you doing here?"

Miguel looked from Betsy to Vivienne. "You want to answer that, Vivi?"

"I believe what we had here last night was a booty call."

"A *what?*"

"A booty call. What your generation called a one-night stand."

"I know what a booty call is." She looked at them smugly. "And I'd bet what little's left of my trust fund that isn't what happened here last night."

"No, really, it isn't what you think it is," Miguel protested.

"You two go on thinking that. I know better." Betsy was smiling as she sailed out the door.

"Well, hell." Miguel finished off the bagel.

"Hell's right. Now she's going to pester me endlessly about us getting back together"

"Sorry about that."

She unearthed another bagel and a small carton from the bag. "Hallelujah. There's cream cheese."

They got out plates and Miguel made himself coffee. They found themselves again sitting side by side at the breakfast bar. "So what are we going to do about the elephant sitting over there on the sofa?" she asked as she spread cream cheese on a bagel.

"Which one? The Durango or the wild night in your bed?" Miguel sipped his coffee and made a face. "You have any creamer or sugar?"

"No creamer. Put in extra sugar. Bowl's in the cabinet."

He dumped in two teaspoons of sugar. "Which elephant are we going to tackle first?"

She sipped her coffee. "We had no business falling into bed together last night. Especially with the other unresolved."

"It wasn't the smartest thing we've ever done. But, hell, I'm not sorry." His gaze was defiant.

"I'm sorry only because it complicates the hell out of the rest of it and solved absolutely nothing." She sighed. "But it was fabulous, I'll give you that."

"And it was anything but empty. Or meaningless." Miguel took her hand. "It was never empty or meaningless for me. I want you to know that."

"Then what was it? We've never been in love with each other."

"Damned if I know. But it meant something. All I know is there's a hole in me that it seems to fill."

"Fair enough." She had no idea what it meant to her. And wasn't sure she wanted to find out.

"So that leaves us the other. I have a proposition for you."

"I'm listening."

"I drop my attempts to persuade you to sell the theater. No more discussions, no more showing it to prospective buyers. Nothing. *Nada.* I won't even bring it up in conversation."

Vivienne eyed him warily. "What do you want in return?"

"I want to spend time with you. I want you to carve out some time in your schedule for me."

"What are you asking for? Sex in exchange for you shutting up about the Durango?"

"It wouldn't be like that. I won't lie—I want to spend more time in your bed. But I'd like other things besides sex. I've missed you. We used to enjoy one another's company. I'd like to enjoy your company again."

"You hated my company at the end. You were relieved when I moved out."

"Only because we were fighting so much." He looked her in the eye. "I'm lonely, Vivi."

"You're horny."

"That too. But I am lonely. It would be nice to take you out for dinner or drop by here with takeout and binge something on Netflix, then split another sack of bagels for breakfast."

"To what end? Where do you see this heading?"

"No particular end, and I have no expectation that it would be heading anywhere. Maybe I'd like to enjoy the good part of what we had without the bad. We could do that. At least for a while." He took her hand in his. "I know you've missed me in your bed because you said so. Tell, me, have you missed anything else we shared? Or was it all about the sex?"

"Of course it wasn't all about the sex." She was stung and didn't try to hide it. "We had a lot of fun together before it went south."

"So? Want to have some more fun? At least until the play is over and we have to make a decision about the theater."

On one hand the whole idea of it was fucking stupid. They had hurt each other. Badly. And, most likely, would hurt one another again. And they still hadn't come to an agreement about the theater. They would be putting off making a decision until the end of the play's run, at which point they would be at loggerheads again. Nothing good was going to come of it.

But… maybe he had a point. She had been lonely since the divorce, and when they weren't fighting, Miguel was great company. They could have a good time together without the baggage of trying to hold together a marriage, at least until the show closed.

And more nights like last night would go a long way to taking the edge off.

Vivienne wasn't a stupid woman. She would have to guard her heart, as she had during their ill-fated marriage. The last thing she needed was to fall in love with Miguel. He had never loved her, he didn't love her now, and, most likely, he never would.

As long as she kept her head on her shoulders and her heart locked away, spending time with Miguel could be enjoyable. She knew it would be pleasurable.

She looked at him and smiled. "Mr. Abonce, you have yourself a deal." She grinned. "You want to spend a little of that time with me this morning?"

"You know, Ms. Heiser, I do believe I would."

***

Miguel whistled under his breath as he unlocked his front door. Damn, the things Vivi did to him in bed. He'd thought she'd wrung him dry last night, but he'd risen to the occasion twice this morning before she'd cooked him a huge second breakfast.

He'd lost the entire morning to her and great sex. Now he'd have to scramble to catch up on the backlog of emails and paperwork before he had to report to the theater for tonight's performance. He'd promised himself he'd get up early and get it finished before the Sunday afternoon matinee. Yeah, well, he didn't regret one moment of his time with Vivi.

She had promised to have dinner with him after tomorrow's show at his favorite Riverwalk restaurant and had suggested they enjoy dessert afterward at her place.

He was expecting more than flan.

Damn. He was crazy. And she had to be just as *loca*. Nothing had changed in their lives. She was still over-the-top obsessed with the Durango. He was still a driven workaholic. They were still at odds over the fate of the theater. And to top it all off, her company was on the verge of bankruptcy.

He didn't know what in the hell they were thinking.

But, fuck it. He was looking forward to the next few weeks like a geek who landed the head cheerleader.

***

Vivienne put the last touches on her makeup and surveyed herself in the mirror. Not too bad, since she hadn't gone to sleep until late and had gotten up again at eight to shower and dress and be across town for an eleven a.m. wedding at Our Lady of the Lake University. One of Miguel's oldest friends was finally tying the knot and Miguel was the best man. She'd been surprised when he'd insisted she come, not only to the evening reception, but to the wedding itself.

In the way of many traditional San Antonio weddings, the church wedding would take place early in the day and the guests would reassemble somewhere else in the evening for a lively party, complete with *barbacoa*, beer, a mariachi band, and lots of dancing.

Tonight's party was being held in the old neighborhood where the groom and Miguel grew up, in a big party room behind their old parish church, and not too far from downtown San Antonio and the theater. She and Miguel agreed to change into their party clothes at the theater and go straight to the reception from there.

She grabbed a lightweight sweater to throw over her dress, a simple silk in fuchsia that highlighted her hair and skin tone. The March wind blew her hair and tossed the falling oak leaves across the sidewalk and into the grille of her car. She whisked out the worst of them and climbed behind the wheel. It was too cool and windy to put the top down, but she opened the windows a little to let in the brisk morning air.

She yawned widely and hoped the cool air would add a bump to the three cups of coffee she'd downed before leaving. She and Miguel had been at it half the night, and he'd told her to sleep when he slipped out at six, but the bed felt too empty after he left.

Despite the fun they were having, she wouldn't bet the scrap metal behind Heiser Steel that they would still be seeing one another come summer. Not with the decision facing them about the Durango. She hadn't changed her mind about keeping the theater. As far as she knew, he hadn't changed his mind about selling it. They had kept to the agreement not to discuss the future of the theater. If his feelings had changed, she wasn't aware, but she doubted that to be the case.

The wind whipped her skirt as she climbed the steps to the beautiful and ornate chapel. The sanctuary was filling rapidly as she slipped into a pew close to the back on the groom's side. Miguel's mother and grandmother were seated closer to the front, and she wasn't sure they would welcome her joining them. Neither of them had taken the divorce well, and she had no idea if Miguel had told them he was spending most of his nights in her bed, and a surprising number of his daytime hours in her company. When she'd agreed to spend time with him, she'd assumed with his busy schedule it would mostly consist of late-night booty calls. But he was a regular visitor to Heiser Steel at noon, and a few times he'd shown up early in the morning with breakfast tacos. More than once he'd appeared at her door around dinnertime with some tempting takeout that they ate in front of the TV before they tumbled into bed.

Vivienne settled back into the pew to enjoy the spectacle of ten bridesmaids, an equal number of groomsmen, a bevy of flower girls and ring bearers. The front of the church was filled to the brim by the time the bride came down the aisle on her brother's arm.

Vivienne spotted Miguel in the crowd, but from this distance she couldn't see the expression on his face. She wondered if he was remembering their wedding the way she was. There was little in here to remind Vivienne of hers, yet her thoughts kept returning to the afternoon she'd made her vows to Miguel in the big Methodist church in the heart of Alamo Heights. Even though she and Miguel had married for reasons other than love, she'd taken her vows seriously. She'd had every intention of living honorably with him for the rest of her life.

She watched with hooded eyes as the mousy bride and balding groom took their vows. Their faces shone with love and joy as they held hands in front of the priest. Vivi and Miguel hadn't looked at one another that way the afternoon they joined their lives. They'd looked at one another with lust, at best. And lust hadn't been enough to hold them together.

As Vivienne stood for the closing prayer, she knew she wouldn't make the same mistake again. She would have this interlude with Miguel, enjoy his company during the day and revel in the passion at night. She might even buy a bigger bed. But she wouldn't be standing up in front of the minister with him again. The next time she made vows, if she ever did, she was going to look at her groom with the kind of love the bride had on her face this morning. And the groom, whoever he might be, was going to look at her the same way.

She started to wait for Miguel, but he texted that the pictures were going to take forever and said he'd meet her back at her place. She was down the steps and out on the sidewalk when she spotted her former mother-in-law trying to help Miguel's grandmother negotiate the uneven walkway with her walker. The old lady's steps were unsteady and Juliana seemed worried. Vivienne trotted down the sidewalk to where the two women were struggling. "Morning," she said brightly, ignoring the scowl on Ximena's face. "This sidewalk's a mess, isn't it? Is there anything I can do to help?"

Juliana's face split into a wide smile. "*Hola, mija. Como estas*?" She enveloped Vivienne in a huge hug. "Oh, I've missed you, *mija*."

"I've missed you, too." Vivienne felt tears sting her eyes as she returned Juliana's hug. "How have you been?"

"I have been wonderful. I love the new house Mico moved us to."

"I'm so glad." She turned and offered her hand to Ximena. "And how are you, Mrs. Torres?" She'd never called Ximena by anything other than her formal name.

Ximena nodded. "*Muy bien. Gracias.* Yourself?"

"I'm doing well. Can I see you two ladies to your car?"

"I have a better idea. Why don't I go get my car and you wait with Mama and make sure she doesn't fall down."

"I'd be glad to. Would you like to sit until Juliana gets back with the car?" Ximena's walker was equipped with a padded chair.

"I could do that." The old lady seated herself carefully. "We have seen little of Miguel lately."

Oh, boy. How much had Miguel told them about their arrangement? "I understand. Three shows a week takes a lot of time. He's probably scrambling to keep up with his paperwork. I know I am."

The old lady looked at her shrewdly. "He also told his mama he was spending time with you again. That you are having—how you say? An affair now. His mama is happy. She thinks you and Miguel will be married again."

"So does mine," Vivienne admitted. "That would be highly unlikely." She looked at Ximena's sour expression and wondered what would come out of the lady's mouth next.

"My Mico, he is lonely." She grabbed Vivienne's arm in a viselike grip. "Don't hurt my Mico again. You leave, he hurt bad. Don't hurt him again, Vivienne. Please."

"It was never my intent to hurt him." She looked at Ximena. "It hurt me, too, ma'am. Please know that."

Ximena nodded once and they waited in silence for Juliana to bring the car around. The old lady was as sharp as ever. She knew they were playing with fire. Sooner or later they were bound to be hurt. Again. But Vivienne didn't have the strength to break things off. There was no way she could give up those precious hours with him.

And, surprisingly, she doubted Miguel could give her up.

***

Vivienne clung to Miguel in the dimly lit party room's dance floor, the deep thrum of the bass guitar vibrating down her body as they drifted together around the big space. It was after one in the morning. The bride and groom were long gone and the older guests and families with children were no longer in attendance. But the younger guests had passed the hat and collected enough money to persuade the band to play for another hour.

It had been nearly eleven by the time Miguel and Vivi had gotten to the party, but the bride's mother had saved generous plates of *barbacoa* with beans and rice, as well as huge slabs of wedding cake that they'd washed down with paper cups filled with Corona from a keg. Then they'd taken to the dance floor.

One of the first things they'd done when they started dating was to teach each other to dance, and by the time they married Vivienne could do a mean *cumbia* and Miguel could waltz her around the floor. But they'd gotten so busy, him with his business and her with the theater, that dancing fell by the wayside. Vivienne couldn't remember the last time they'd danced together. They should have kept dancing, she thought as he slid her seductively across the floor. They should have made time to dance together at least once in a while.

She was beginning to think they should have made time for a lot of things.

The band brought the sexy number to a close. They played two more and announced it would be their last song. "Shall we dance or leave?" Miguel whispered into her ear.

"We could go home and finish what we started here," she purred, her lips curving in a smile.

They exited the dance floor, and Vivienne gathered up her wrap and her handbag and they headed for the door hand in hand. They were halfway to the car when two grungy-looking thugs jumped out from between two cars, both brandishing Saturday night specials.

"Your purse, your wallet, your jewelry, your phones," they demanded.

Vivienne's heart leapt to her throat. This close, those cheapie guns would kill. She glanced over at Miguel. His lips were flattened into a tight line but he was otherwise expressionless as he fished his wallet out of his back pocket. Vivienne's fingers trembled as she handed over her clutch. "Phone?" the thug asked. She nodded toward the handbag. "Jewelry too, lady. A rich bitch like you wears the real thing."

Not tonight, asshole. She fought to keep her lips from twitching as she removed her costume choker from around her neck and made herself look appropriately distressed as she handed it over. The little shit was going to get a rude shock when he went to pawn it. A glance over at Miguel had her groaning for real. He was handing over the Rolex her father had given him the first Christmas they were married.

The thieves took off running with their booty. Miguel grabbed her by the hand and they sprinted back to the party room, where the band was still playing. "Damn, we should have kept dancing," Miguel snapped. She was shaking too hard to do anything but nod.

They borrowed a phone and Miguel called in the robbery. A bored-looking officer showed up thirty minutes later as the band was loading the last of their equipment into an old van. The policeman took a report, told them to get their licenses replaced as soon as they could, and instructed them not to get pulled over on the drive home.

"Fucking help he was," Miguel ground out as the patrol car took off.

"At least you have your car keys," she pointed out, earning a blistering glare. "He could have demanded those too. And you'd be down a Lexus."

"What a fucking comfort."

Okaaay. He was going to be rude and surly and unreasonable about the whole thing.

They were quiet on the way to her condo. Miguel followed her inside and threw himself on the sofa. "Fucking crap-ass place to have a wedding reception. Whole fucking neighborhood's crap-ass."

"You want something to drink?"

"No, I don't want something to drink. How the hell can you be so calm? You lost a God-damn diamond choker, for Christ's sake."

"I lost a nice costume piece I wore in *Pippin*. I'm sorry as hell you lost the Rolex. And as for calm?" She held out her fingers. "I'm still shaking. I was scared." She took a deep breath. "We could have been killed."

"That's for damned sure. I don't know why in the hell Tommy couldn't have had the party downtown or in one of the country clubs where that kind of shit doesn't go down. Why go back to that fucking dump of a neighborhood?"

"Dunno." She went to the kitchen and poured herself a glass of wine with hands that weren't quite steady. "Sentimental reasons, maybe. Fond memories of where he grew up. Besides, that kind of thing happens all over town, not only in the barrio. It could have happened just as easily downtown or two blocks from here."

"That's horse shit and you know it." Miguel jumped up and stomped across the room. "That neighborhood sucks and has since I grew up in it. Why do you think I moved Mama and *Abuelita* away? Oh, that's right. You wouldn't know. You grew up in the fancy part of town. You didn't have gangs roaming the streets day and night and drive-bys happening on the next block. Hell, the policemen in your little enclave have so little to do they leave tickets on cars parked in the wrong direction on the street." He glared across the room at her. "You have no fucking idea what it was like, living with drugs and violence right outside the fucking window. It *could* happen anywhere. It *does* happen in that shit-pile of a neighborhood, on a regular damned basis."

Vivienne looked at him and shook her head. "Yeah, my neighborhood was real safe. Which is why Mom was carjacked in the driveway my senior year of high school." She looked at Miguel with exasperation. "Is this where you go off on me because I grew up rich and you didn't? I had so much more than you and had it so much better than you, and poor you had to work for everything he ever had while spoiled little Vivi had it all handed to her on a silver platter? If it is, stuff a cork in it and go home. It's nearly three and I don't feel like listening to one of your dumb-shit, unfounded, totally ridiculous insecurity-induced tirades."

Miguel froze in his tracks. "Is that what you think? That this is about insecurity?"

"Oh, absolutely. You had several of these meltdowns while we were married, usually triggered by some bullshit like tonight. *Mijo pobrecito*, grew up in the barrio and had it so damned rough. Well, tough shit. Yep, you grew up poor and had to work your butt off. And look where it got you. You're a rich man. You're the West Side Wunderkind. You can buy pretty much anything you want. Unlike some of us, your company is in great shape. I get that your childhood wasn't the best in the world, but hell's bells, Miguel, hasn't your fucking wonderful dream-come-true adulthood made up for it?"

He looked at her belligerently. "I'm pissed about being robbed. And yeah, sometimes I resent the hell out of growing up in that neighborhood and never having two nickels to rub together. That doesn't mean I'm insecure. And I'm not having an insecurity meltdown tonight."

"No, you're sure not. Because I'm not going to listen to one."

"Fuck you. It wouldn't hurt you to be a little sympathetic."

"Why, when you don't need one single scrap of sympathy?" Her lips tightened. "I get that I had an easier childhood than you did. I would be the first to admit that I was given a lot. But you had some great things, too. Some things I didn't have. You had two bright, strong, level-headed women raising you. You want to trade either of them for Betsy? You had two wonderful men who loved you. Big Mike Abonce started you down the right path and Tripp Heiser took over when you lost your dad. Do you ever think to be grateful for that? Or do you look at the rundown neighborhood and shabby little house you grew up in and think you have a pity party coming?"

Miguel's eyes flamed. "I am not having a pity party."

"Don't know what else you'd call it. You amaze me sometimes. You have earned so much, achieved so much, accomplished so damn much, and yet sometimes you turn right back into that kid from the barrio and think you're still standing on the outside looking in. When are you going to realize you came inside a long time ago?"

"I haven't come inside, not really. And as long as my last name's Abonce and not Smith or Heiser, I never will. And, as a Heiser you'll never understand that."

He shouldered past her and slammed the door on the way out.

Well. This certainly wasn't the way she'd envisioned ending the day.

Vivienne sighed and downed the rest of the wine. She wasn't surprised. Miguel could be sensitive sometimes about his youth and his background. Never mind how many times she assured him that he'd arrived, and that he was every bit as highly regarded as any other businessman in San Antonio. In his eyes he was still that kid from the wrong part of town sitting at Tripp Heiser's desk for the first time, wanting with all his heart to be like the businessman he admired so much.

Vivienne cringed at the anger on Miguel's face as he'd slammed out of here tonight. She'd been hard on him. And should have been more compassionate. For the first time, she saw things through his eyes. He was right. She'd never understand what it would be feel like to be Latina. To feel like she was on the outside looking in. Even in San Antonio, where sixty-three percent of the population was of Latino origin, the money and the power in the city had been held tightly in the hands of white folks for a long, long time.

Maybe she needed to tell him that.

Chapter Eight

Miguel pulled into the parking lot across from the Durango. His head pounded from a lack of sleep and the whiskey he'd downed in the wee hours of the morning. He'd overslept and hadn't dealt with the pile of paperwork on his desk. And, thanks to having to work two shows today, the adult matinee and the teenage production this evening, the pile would have to sit until tomorrow.

He ran his hand around his neck and cursed the hammers beating between his eyes. Between the time crewing the show and all the time he was spending with Vivi, the after-hours time he usually devoted to his business had dropped off drastically. If he and Vivi continued their relationship after the play finished its run, he was going to have to cut back on the time he was spending with his ex-wife or hire a paper shuffler. But he would hold off making that hire until after the show. If Vivienne was forced to sell the Durango, she was going to hold him responsible, and would most likely show him to the door.

If she wasn't planning to do that already. Miguel stood at the corner, waiting for the light to change, and cursed that he had exploded last night. He had taken out his frustration—and, yeah, fear—on her. While she'd never lorded her family's wealth or social status over him, and had proudly introduced him to her friends and the business contacts he sought so eagerly, she couldn't know what he felt and had lived. She had never treated him as inferior in any way, but she never understood the feeling either.

But she was wrong about one thing. Maybe he'd been on the inside during their marriage, but the divorce had closed some doors that had been open while Tripp Heiser's daughter was his wife. Not many, but enough for him to confirm that there was and always would be a social divide in his hometown. No matter how much money he made, how successful he became, he would never be totally accepted by the wealthy Anglo community, unless he remarried Vivienne, or made another advantageous marriage into their circle.

He owed Vivi an apology, big time. She'd been mugged, too, and was still shaking when he went off on her. She didn't deserve what he dished out last night. She'd always forgiven him during their marriage. But they weren't married anymore, and he had no idea if she would forgive him this time.

He pushed open the lobby doors to the theater and wandered in. He was a little early and the lobby was deserted but for Stanley, who was already working behind the concession counter. Stanley threw up his hand in greeting and went back to whatever he was doing. Miguel walked through the lobby and was about to go through the theater to the stage when he heard Vivi's voice coming from the stairwell. "Damn it, Cam, I didn't give the assholes your cell phone number."

Miguel froze. Vivi was seriously upset.

"Then how did they get it?" Cameron sounded furious.

"Collection agencies have any number of ways to get a cell phone number. You know that."

Collection agency? What the hell was going on? Cameron Heiser was the last man who would be irresponsible with his credit.

"Fine. Sorry I jumped you. It just pisses me off. The SOBs called me at seven this morning. That damned supplier in Arkansas turned us in even after we made a partial payment last week."

"Well, hell. Word gets out we have a collection agency after us Heiser Steel won't be able to get credit from anybody. Jesus, Cam, am I gonna have to sell this place to save the company? Am I gonna have to let the Durango go?" The anguish in her voice was heartbreaking.

"I don't know." Cameron's voice was thick. "Aw, Vivi, don't cry. Something's gonna give, I swear it. Now dry those eyes and go turn yourself into Reno Sweeney."

Miguel darted into the men's room. He didn't want Vivienne to know he'd overheard them. But damn. If it was so bad that their creditors were turning to collection agencies to get their money, Heiser Steel was in worse shape than he'd realized. The door swung open and Cameron hustled inside, his eyes shimmering with tears. He grabbed a paper towel out of the dispenser and looked at Miguel. "How much did you hear?" He dabbed at his eyes.

"Enough."

Cameron sniffed. "I feel like I let her down."

"It wasn't you. At least she's beginning to realize she's probably going to have to sell."

Cameron glared at him. "Thrills your soul, doesn't it?"

"No, it doesn't. I hurt for her, as hard as that may be for you to believe." He slammed out of the restroom before Cameron could answer.

He had to give Vivienne her due. By the time the rest of the cast and the crew showed up, she had pulled herself together and delivered yet another fabulous performance. But she ducked out the minute she was through shaking hands with the audience. Cameron left a couple of minutes later.

With two hours on his hands before the teen production, Miguel crossed the street and treated himself to a huge plate of enchiladas at the restaurant in Market Square. Not as good as his mom's, but almost.

The high school cast was assembling when he returned. A teenaged girl dressed as Evangeline Harcourt was stringing a hairline mic into Sophie Aldrete's dark, elaborately styled tresses while Letti took surreptitious peeks into the dressing room. "She's playing it as a brunette," he observed.

"Ethel Merman played it as a brunette in the original production." Letti bit her lip. "Do you suppose they need help?"

"They have it under control, Mama. And don't you have a clipboard full of stuff to take care of?"

She nodded sheepishly and wandered off. The only grownups backstage were him and some other members of the adult crew. And they wouldn't be there for long. Once the adult crew reviewed their respective responsibilities with the teenaged crew, they exited the stage and found seats upstairs in the balcony. Miguel noted that there was no band tonight. The kids were using a canned soundtrack. Letti slipped in at the last minute and sat down beside him. "It's strange backstage. There is not one adult back there. Not. One."

"And the kids manage to pull it off with no supervision?"

She grinned proudly. "Watch."

At first he watched with curiosity and then with growing admiration and amazement as the play unfolded to an appreciative audience of family and friends. The makeup jobs were perfect, including the skillful application of aging makeup for the kids playing the older roles. There was no stumbling over lines, no singing gaffes, no slips of any kind that would give away the tender ages of the cast. Letti assured him the kids were behaving in a totally adult manner backstage. "If they can't pull it off, they're not cast," she said.

In short, he was blown away.

"Are they this good every time?" he asked as he and Letti sipped sodas during intermission.

"Absolutely. Even the little ones turn in top-notch performances. Now, with them we do have a few adults backstage."

"You'd told me that some are from the barrio," he said slowly.

"Some, yes. Quite a few, actually."

He eyed the stage thoughtfully. "I wonder if there would be any way to expand the program to include more barrio kids. A program like this would open so many doors for children from impoverished backgrounds."

Letti looked at him shrewdly. "Yes, it would. Absolutely. But, like a lot of other good things, it all boils down to money. Programs like this one don't come cheap. And with the fate of the theater in jeopardy, nobody's too worried about expanding the scholarship program." She glanced in his direction. "Vivi said the situation at Heiser Steel is dire. She's terrified she's going to have to make a choice. Whatever she decides is going to break her heart." She looked at him pointedly.

"I'm rich, but not that rich. I can't rescue Heiser Steel for them. I wish I could." He sighed. "Letti, the bottom line is that she can't eat her cake and have it too. Either the theater goes or Heiser Steel goes. Simple as that."

"Which isn't simple at all."

"No, it really isn't."

***

It was almost eleven by the time he got to Vivi's condo. The lights were on and through the translucent shades he could see more than one person moving around. He started to leave, but he really needed to tell her he was sorry for last night. He took the steps two at a time and knocked briskly. Vivienne jerked open the door, wearing her old robe and an expression that meant she was already irked about something. "Come on in. Last night it was you. Tonight it's Mom and Aunt Katie's turn."

He followed Vivienne into her living room. Betsy and Katie Heiser were sitting together on the sofa with a high-end cruise line magazine in front of them and pouts on their faces. "Honestly, I don't see what the problem is," Katie said balefully. "It's not anywhere near what the trip to Europe would have cost."

"No. It's a fifteen-day cruise through the Panama Canal with the most expensive cruise line out there," Vivienne snapped. "Why are we having this discussion again? The Heiser family is on a tight budget for the foreseeable future."

"But it's not that much, honestly," Betsy argued. "Tripp would have taken me on the trip without thinking twice about it."

"And I went on this kind of cruise all the time during summer vacation. I even paid for some of them myself," Katie said proudly.

Vivienne and Miguel shared a look. Katie had worked part-time as a music teacher for an exclusive academy that paid their teachers a fraction of what public school teachers made. The money she'd lived on all her life was from Heiser Steel.

"That may be so, but you're hardly in a position to pay for it now," Vivienne explained tiredly. "And the company's not in a position to pick up the tab. Sorry." Her phone rang and her eyes widened. "Shit. It's the same collection agency that called Cameron this morning. Sorry, I better take this." She jumped up out of her chair and started up the stairs. "Yes, this is Vivienne Heiser. How did you get this number?" They heard her shut her bedroom door.

"Collection agency? Why would a collection agency be calling Vivienne at eleven on a Sunday night?" Betsy asked, genuinely dumbfounded.

"That's when collection agencies call. Early in the morning or late at night, even though it's illegal to call before or after eight. They try to catch people at their most vulnerable," he told them.

"But why would they be calling Cameron and Vivienne at all?"

"Something to do with the company?" Katie asked quietly, quicker on the uptake than her sister-in-law.

"Apparently, one of their suppliers turned them over to an agency when they couldn't pay their whole bill. They called Cameron this morning early. Now they're pestering her." He gestured to the brochure. "The last thing she needs right is for the two of you to worry her by coming up with more ways to spend company money. She has enough on her plate, don't you think?"

"Goodness, we never meant to worry her," Betsy said. "But it's not that expensive, honestly." She opened the magazine and handed it to him.

He looked at the price and whistled. "It is expensive, by anyone's standards."

"If you say so." She took the magazine from him. "But we haven't gone anywhere or done anything in ages. I thought it would be a nice little trip."

"Bored?" he asked.

Betsy thought a minute. "Kind of."

"More than kind of," Katie said. "There's only so much volunteering one can do."

"I see." He paused. How could he suggest this delicately? "Have you ever considered getting jobs? That would take care of the boredom and at the same time help out with the money."

Katie shrugged. "I worked a lot of years. I have no desire to go back."

"Even if it would help?" he went on.

"I worked. I'm done. I'm not going back." Katie was sticking to her guns.

He turned to Betsy. "What about you? Have you ever thought about getting a job?"

She lifted her chin. "The only job I ever held in my life was to be Mrs. Tripp Heiser. That's the only thing I know how to do. Unfortunately, there isn't much demand for that skill set in the job market."

She had a point.

Vivienne came downstairs, her lips tight and two spots of red on her cheeks. "Well, that was fun."

Betsy picked up the magazine and she and Katie stood. "We've taken enough of your time. I didn't mean to upset you, dear. I hope you know that."

"I know. See you both later."

Betsy and Katie swept out the door, as regal as queens. Vivi sank down into the sofa and put her head in her hands. "God deliver me from those two. What ways will they think up next to run through money?"

Miguel sat down beside her and put his arm around her shoulders. "They're bored. I told them they needed to get jobs. They didn't quite know what to do with that."

"I can imagine. Mom never worked a day in her life. Aunt Katie put in three whole hours a day. Sad part is that at their ages and with the lack of a salable skill, even if they wanted to work, I doubt anyone would hire either of them." She rubbed her tired-looking eyes. "So what brings you here tonight?"

"A much-deserved apology. From me to you. I was a total ass last night and I'm sorry. Every time I have to go back there, I turn into that kid with cheap athletic shoes, a hoodie that wasn't warm enough, and a cop looking at me with suspicion."

Vivienne winced visibly. "I'm sorry it makes you feel that way. But you're hardly that kid anymore."

He shifted on the sofa. "Some of those doors you opened for me closed after the divorce. Businessmen who were perfectly willing to deal with Tripp Heiser's son-in-law weren't interested in the West Side Wunderkind."

Vivienne raised an eyebrow. "Some of Daddy's former business associates are assholes. This is news to you because…?"

He smiled ruefully. "Shouldn't be, I guess. Anyway, is my apology for being a total ass last night accepted?"

"Of course. I wish you could see yourself through my eyes." She smiled. "And, I want to apologize, too." Miguel's brow went up. "You're right. I could never understand what it feels like to be treated as less than because of the color of my skin or my heritage."

"Thank you for that. It means more than you could know." As he squeezed her hand something in his chest unlatched. Released. And he felt lighter. "And, I wish you could see yourself through my eyes. You've never thought of yourself as an attractive woman. But you are. No one's a super model, even them. Vivi, you have something special I don't know how to put into words, but it's a quality that is compelling."

"That's me acting. Like when I become Reno Sweeney."

"No, that's me looking at Vivienne Heiser. I've always seen this in you even though you don't."

She smiled. "That's lovely of you. My beat-up ego says thanks."

"You're more than welcome." He pulled her to him and planted a kiss on her lips. "Now, do you accept my apology and I go home, or do you accept my apology and I spend the night holding onto you?"

"You could do more than hold onto me." She ran her hand down the side of his face.

"You're not too tired?"

Her smile was sultry. "I am never too tired for that. You know better, Miguel."

"Just making sure, *querida*." He met her gaze and saw the truth there. The need. The longing. The desire. For him.

At moments like this, he did see himself through her eyes. And she made him feel ten feet tall.

He met her lips in a kiss he hope conveyed everything he felt. He wanted Vivi to see herself through his eyes the way he could see himself through hers. He wanted her to envision the sensual, fascinating woman he saw when he looked at her, both on stage and off. He wanted her to see the Vivi that rocked his world and sweated up the sheets. He wanted her to see that she was everything he wanted in a woman.

He wanted her to see how much he desired her.

His lips brushed hers, and as they edged closer the kiss deepened. Miguel's heart pounded in his throat as their tongues met and went into battle for dominance. She tasted of coffee and mint and that indefinable something that was Vivi. He reveled in her touch as she ran her fingers through his hair. He wrapped his arms around her and held her close, breathing in the fragrance that made his heart beat faster and his breath catch in his throat. It felt fresh and new tonight. But then it always did. Even though they had done this hundreds of times, he felt like something new was happening every time he touched her.

He took his time kissing her, every kiss deeper than the last. He'd been hard as a rock from the moment she'd squeezed his hand. His fingers went on one of his favorite journeys over her lithe curves—her nape, her back, her breasts, and her slender waist. He took his time. Her breath hitched and her nipples strained through the thin fabric of the threadbare robe. He undid the sash and pushed it off her shoulders. "I need to get you a new one of these," he murmured against her lips.

"Do I need to get you some more of those sexy silk boxers?" she teased as he deftly removed her pajama top, baring her to her waist.

"Uh-huh." He put his hands in the waistband of her pajama bottoms. "Everything off." He yanked down the bottoms. "Now, that's how I like you." He ran his hands down her side and settled them on her hips. "Naked and beautiful." He swept her up in his arms and made it up the stairs in record time.

As he put her down next to the bed, she purred, "But this isn't how I like you." She pouted. "You are way too covered up." She reached down and then jerked his T-shirt over his head. "That's more like it," she breathed as she ran her fingers through the hair on his chest. "But you need to keep going."

He grinned as he shucked his jeans and boxers. She eyed his underwear. "We gotta find those sexy silk ones," she muttered. "Oh, my." She fingered his jutting cock and pulled the boxers down. "On the other hand, whatever you're wearing is fine."

He laughed and pulled her down on the bed beside him. They held each other for long moments, kissing and touching, letting the passion build. His lips were on her breasts, hers were on his neck and his chest. He palmed her stomach and felt her quiver beneath his caress. His hand drifted lower, to the junction between her thighs. "Open up," he commanded. "I want more."

Obediently she shifted her legs. He began exploring, taking his time as he found and caressed her petals and core. Her breath hitched and she made the soft, mewling sounds he adored as he stroked her the way she loved for him to. Her harsh gasps and labored breathing told him she was nearing climax, and he drew out the pleasure until she called out his name as she bucked with passion. He gave her a few long moments before resuming his tender assault, sliding down her body and staking his claim with his lips and tongue. His cock throbbed as he again led her up and over again. The taste of her was on his lips as he eased himself between her legs. "Are you ready?"

"Are you kidding?" She clasped his hips with her legs and locked her ankles behind him. "I was ready two orgasms ago."

He slid into her with a single stroke. "Ahh, feels like I'm coming home," he breathed. He was still for a moment, savoring their intimate connection before beginning to move within her. She countered his motion, meeting his thrusts and clasping his hips with her legs. Together they soared.

Blood pounded in Miguel's ears as the tension built between them, climbing toward release. Vivi arched in his arms as her climax broke and he stiffened and thrust into her as a powerful orgasm overtook him, his cock throbbing within her as he came. They clung to each other as delicious aftershocks continued to reverberate between them.

Without leaving her body, Miguel twisted so that they lay facing one another. "It was so good, *querida*," he whispered as he brushed his lips against hers.

"It's always good." She snuggled closer.

He eased out of her and turned over on his back, bringing her with him. She snuggled in close. "Gonna be up for round two in a few?"

She nodded sleepily, but within minutes her breathing shifted to soft, whiffling snores. Miguel kissed her forehead. He was a little disappointed that she'd dropped off, but after being up most of the night, and with the difficult day she'd had, he could understand her fatigue.

He was tired, too, but sleep eluded him as he thought why, since they'd begun sleeping together again, sex had been better than ever. And now he was feeling things he hadn't felt before. He burned for her in a way he hadn't in the past. He needed her. He wanted to wrap his arms around her and hold her close. He wanted more than a woman with the right connections.

He wanted all of Vivienne. He hadn't before. But he did now.

He didn't want to examine the whys of needing her and wanting her this way. It didn't make a difference why. It just was.

He knew what he wanted.

He wanted her back.

He wanted her in his bed and by his side.

He wanted to talk to her in the morning and to come home to her in the evening.

He wanted to share his innermost thoughts with her.

And when he wanted something that badly, he moved heaven and earth until he got it.

He was going to win her back.

Whatever it took, she was going to be his once again.

Chapter Nine

A balmy April breeze tossed Miguel's hair into disarray as he pulled his convertible into the parking lot across from the Durango. He hit the button to raise the top and laid his sunglasses on the console. He checked his watch. There was time for a taco run. Twenty minutes later he was hiding in what he thought of as his spot in the balcony munching down on rich, spicy *carne guisada* wrapped in a soft flour tortilla. The taco was good, almost as good as his mother's, and he realized with a shock that he would miss picking them up at the café across the street and hiding up here to eat them when the play finished its run.

He would miss a lot of things when the show ended.

Wasn't that a kicker? Miguel Abonce, a dyed-in-the-wool cynical workaholic, had actually enjoyed the time spent volunteering backstage for a community theater production. Vivienne would be surprised, stunned even, if he admitted it, especially after all the complaining he'd done and the fights they'd had. Parts of what he'd done, and seen, had been a lot of fun, and he was beginning to understand why Vivienne thought it so important that the Durango stay alive.

He finished the tacos and ambled down the stairs. The actors were beginning to wander in and Stanley was busy behind the concessions counter. Vivienne, Jessica, and Miranda were grouped around Jessica's cell phone. "Oh, wow," Vivienne crowed. "I can't believe it." She motioned to Wade, who was coming through the lobby. "Hey, come take a look. Sandra's husband bought her a theater. She sent pictures of the renovations she's overseeing."

Wade smiled crookedly. "She sent them to me, too. The hillbilly turned out to be a decent dude after all."

"She wouldn't have gone back to him if he hadn't," Jessica said. Wade nodded and wandered off and Jessica kept scrolling. "Oh, look. Here's a picture of Noelle. Gosh, she's grown since they left."

"You feed 'em, they grow." Miranda laughed. "Hey, Miguel. Come take a look. Sandra's husband went in with his brothers and bought her the Sullivan and Company Theater in Johnson City. He gave it to her for Christmas and she's in the process of renovating it. She's hoping to put on their first production this coming summer."

Miguel leaned over and peered at the screen. A vaguely familiar blonde posed in front of an old theater beside the beautiful child who'd played the head Munchkin last fall. "Where do I know her from?"

"You probably saw her perform a couple of times. She played Dorothy in *The Wizard of Oz*. It was her last production before she took Noelle back to Tennessee and reconciled with her husband. He's gone a lot with his band and wanted her to have something she loved as much as he loves singing." Vivienne looked wistfully at the picture. "I bet she's in heaven."

Miguel motioned with his hand and Jessica flipped through a few of the pictures. "How'd he afford it?" he asked.

"He and the brothers are in a hot country band from Nashville," Jessica said. "They're making plenty and wanted an investment. They picked it up for a fraction of what one would cost here in San Antonio."

"Especially one sitting on prime downtown real estate," Miranda added dryly. "Must be nice. Oh, well. It's time for me to get to work."

"Same here. Gotta go turn into Hope. You coming, Vivienne?"

"I told Josh I'd greet the kids on the bus before I went backstage." She glanced down at her watch. "I hope the bus gets here in a couple of minutes. It takes me a little while to turn into Reno."

Miguel glanced toward the lobby. "I think you're in luck. A big yellow school bus just pulled up. Why the special effort to meet them ahead of time?"

"This is the drama club from Thoreau High. Josh thought it would be good PR to introduce them to the star." She did air quotes around "the star." "Maggie thinks she can land us a grant for Academy tuition for some of them and Josh wants to get them interested in coming this summer."

Thoreau High. His alma mater. "Do you mind if I stay and greet them also?" he asked quietly.

"I forgot, you graduated from Thoreau." She grinned mischievously. "Do I introduce you as the West Side Wunderkind or plain old Mr. Abonce?"

It turned out that no introductions were necessary. The drama club sponsor took one look at Miguel and ran up to shake his hand. "Miguel Abonce, how are you? You've made us all so proud. Every time your company gets a mention in the business section the faculty indulges in a round of 'we knew him when.'"

Miguel laughed. "I'm flattered. So how are you, Mr. Neuwirth? When did you start teaching drama?"

"I'm doing wonderfully. I took over the drama department four years ago and hope to get some of my more promising students involved in your Academy."

"It's my understanding that the powers that be here are hoping for the same. And speaking of"—he turned to Vivienne—"here's the star of this afternoon's production ready to meet your students. Vivienne is playing Reno Sweeney."

"I'm so glad to meet you, Mr. Neuwirth." Vivienne shook his hand before turning to the students milling around behind him. "Welcome to the Durango," she said to the gawking teenagers. "We're so glad you came this afternoon. Let me tell you a bit about the musical you're going to see." She gave them a quick rundown of the history of Cole Porter and *Anything Goes,* then asked if anyone had a question.

Miguel stifled a chuckle at the starstruck kids in their hoodies and jeans trying so hard to be cool with Vivienne. He'd been that kid once upon a time. His hero had been a businessman, not an actress, but the awe was the same. Josh added his welcome and ushered the students to a block of seats in the back of the theater. Miguel and Vivienne left Josh with the students and Mr. Neuwirth.

"They seem excited to be here," Miguel said as they climbed the side steps to the stage.

"Of course they're excited to be here. For most of them, this is probably their first visit to a live theater. I can hardly wait until after the show to hear what they thought of it."

"You're only looking forward to them bragging on you," he teased.

She winked. "That too."

He peeked out at the students more than once as the show progressed. If the claps, whistles and foot stomping were any indication, the students were loving every minute of the show.

He excused himself for a bit after the final curtain and joined the cast and audience in the lobby. The beaming students were falling all over themselves to shake hands with the cast. "Definitely a hit with the kids," Miguel said to Mr. Neuwirth.

"Oh, it was, big-time," his old teacher agreed. "I hope we can get at least a few of them involved in the summer program here." He glanced around the lobby. "This place is a community treasure. I'm glad you've chosen to become involved."

He stifled a wince. Mr. Neuwirth wouldn't be so proud if he knew the real reason Miguel was here. "Yeah. It's an absolute treasure."

He glanced over at Vivienne and from the expression on her face he knew she'd overheard the teacher's comment and his response. He'd reacted much differently when she'd tried to tell him the same thing.

Miguel was deep in thought as he returned to his backstage duties. Joe's plan had worked. It had taken getting involved with a production, seeing it unfold from start to finish, for Miguel to appreciate what the Durango meant to so many people. The actors, the directors, the crew, the Academy kids, even the appreciative audience. The Durango enriched many lives. Vivienne was right in wanting to save it.

But she and her family would have to give up so much if she did.

He was cleaning out the backstage restroom when Vivienne left the dressing room in jeans and a T-shirt. "Meet me at the condo. You want takeout for supper?" she asked.

"How about we go out to that new Mongolian barbeque place that opened around the corner from you?"

"Works for me." She hesitated. "We need to talk." She bit her lip. "I know we said we'd postpone the discussion until after the show, but..."

"It's okay. We can talk tonight."

His mind whirled as he drove to her place. He wracked his brain for a solution, but none presented themselves. Vivienne met him at the door. She was freshly showered but hadn't bothered with makeup. Tension and fatigue tightened her lips and the flesh around her eyes. "Do you even want to go out, *querida*?" he asked as he ran his hand down the side of her face.

She smiled faintly. "I'm okay. Just tired."

He didn't call her on the lie. He took her by the hand and led her to his car. They were mostly silent on the short drive to the new restaurant. They filled metal bowls with the vegetables and meat of their choice and handed them over to be stir-fried. He filled their cups with iced tea while she gathered up silverware and napkins and claimed a booth in the back of the small dining room. He sat down across from her and handed her one of the cups. "Ahh, that hits the spot," she murmured after a long drink of tea. "Okay. Are we going to talk now or later?"

"Now works for me."

She swallowed and tears filled her eyes. "What do we do, Miguel? You saw those kids this afternoon. It was magic for them."

"It's magic for a lot of people, Vivi. And jobs for ten or fifteen. I get that now. But."

"I know. Heiser Steel. I don't know how it could get any worse for the business. The bank won't lend us any more capital. Either Heiser Steel gets a huge infusion of cash sometime in the next four weeks or we declare bankruptcy and close the doors. Then some lucky investor will buy it for pennies on the dollar."

"How many will lose their jobs?"

"A hundred and fifty, mostly men with families. No matter what we end up doing, keeping the Durango or selling it, somebody gets screwed over royally." She fisted her hand on the table. "I kept thinking Cameron and I could pull a rabbit out of the hat. Like Daddy and Granddaddy did a couple of times."

"They robbed Peter to pay Paul. They took out loans and Tripp raided your mother's trust fund. He used resources he never should have used to bail out the company and cover his bad business decisions, and now you and Cameron are trying to cope with the mess he left you."

Her eyes widened. "You've always thought Tripp Heiser could do no wrong."

He covered her fist with his hand. "I never thought that. I appreciated all he'd done for me." He patted her fisted hand. "So let's look at the options." He held up a finger. "Option one. We keep the theater. Josh and Maggie and all the other employees keep their jobs and the theater keeps doing wonderful things. You and Cameron file for bankruptcy and sell the business. Your employees find other jobs where they may or may not make what they did at Heiser Steel. You and Cameron go to work in the corporate sector. Betsy and Katie either go to work or live on their social security checks."

"Option one sucks."

"Okay then. Option two. You and I sell the theater to Horace Foster or someone like him and split the profits. You save Heiser Steel and get it profitable again. You and Cameron and a hundred-fifty men supporting families get to keep your jobs. The theater is torn down. Josh and Maggie and the rest of the employees lose their jobs and may or may not get a job at another theater. The volunteer participants, yourself included, either find a spot at one of the other theaters in town or give up acting. The kids may find other programs around town to meet their needs."

"Option two sucks." She slammed her fist down on the table. "If only it didn't have to be torn down. If only somebody would buy it, like Sandra's husband did."

"Unfortunately, the Durango's worth a lot more than the theater in Tennessee because of where it's located. It's beyond what a single theater-loving investor can afford. Or even two or three investors, unless they were really rich."

Vivienne thought a minute. "What if it were more than two or three investors? What if it were ten investors, or fifteen or twenty? Or fifty? People who love the theater. People who'd like to see the Durango stay alive. People who'd like the tax break of renting to a nonprofit."

Miguel raised his brow. "And where are you going to find this consortium?"

"You put it together by finding interested investors and persuading them put their money to work."

Miguel looked at her doubtfully. "I don't know, Vivi. It's a long shot."

"I get that. But it's the only option that would save both the company and Heiser Steel." She looked at him pleadingly. "We at least need to try, Miguel."

"Okay. We'll try." He reached across the table and squeezed her hand. "If I'm not mistaken, that's our dinner coming this way."

It *was* a long shot, he thought later as he lay beside Vivi with his hand on her hip. But it was the only shot they had at saving both the theater and the company. He turned over on his side and snuggled up to her.

They would try to assemble a consortium to buy the Durango.

He hoped to hell they succeeded.

For Vivienne's sake. And his own.

***

Assembling a consortium to purchase the Durango was easier said than done. Vivienne hung up the phone and rubbed her temples, hoping she could stave off the tension headache she felt building behind her eyes. It had seemed like such a good idea. A few phone calls to San Antonio movers and shakers, a few minutes to sell the idea, and the money would start rolling in. But she had spent the better part of the last week on the phone and had raised less than a hundred thousand dollars, nowhere near what the Durango would sell for in the downtown real estate market. She sighed and turned to make another call when Betsy came sailing through the door with a big smile on her face. "I've come to steal you away for lunch. And I'm not taking no for an answer. Get your handbag and let's go."

"To what do I owe this visit?" Vivienne asked. Typically, her mother steered clear of the factory.

"Cameron said you're working too hard and getting frazzled. So we're going to that dreadful place next door and you're going to eat tacos and relax. And no, I'm not here to ask you to pay for something else you don't think the company can afford, so you can get that deer in the headlights look off your face and come with me."

"Oh. Sorry." Embarrassed and immensely relieved at the same time, Vivienne found her purse and she and Betsy walked to the café. The owner greeted her by name and led them to the booth that practically had her father's name on it. It was the same booth where she'd been sitting when her father introduced her to Miguel.

Their waitress brought them water and chips and salsa. "So what has you so frazzled that Cameron's calling me to come take you out to lunch?"

"Heiser Steel's down to the wire. We have a little more than three weeks before we get a huge infusion of funds or we shut the doors. I've faced the fact that the theater has to be sold. But Miguel and I figured that if we could put together a consortium of investors, it could be sold to them and still stay open. Miguel and I would still split the profits and I could save the company."

"But?"

"It's not as simple as it sounds. I've spent the better part of the last week on the phone. The problem is that the people who love the theater the most passionately don't have the money to make more than a token investment. And the potential investors with the most money to sink into the Durango aren't that interested. I had one come out and ask me why he'd care about keeping the Durango going, when he can see the touring Broadway productions any time they come to town."

"Ouch."

"Ouch is right."

"Who all have you called?"

Vivienne rattled off a list of names. Betsy looked at her and shook her head. "And you honestly thought they would be interested? Sweetie, you're calling the wrong people."

"I am?"

"You're calling your father's old cronies, who couldn't care less. You don't call them. You call their wives. Most of those ladies have money of their own and very well might be interested."

"But I don't know their wives."

"I do." She shoved a pile of napkins across the table. "Make me a list of the men you've called. I'll call their wives. And their daughters, if they have them."

Vivienne listed the names of the men she'd called. Betsy looked it over and put it in her purse. "This is a start. There are quite a few you didn't think of. I'll call them, too." Betsy reached across the table and patted Vivienne's arm. "We'll get you your consortium, Vivi. We'll save the Durango."

"Thanks, Mom." She looked at Betsy curiously. "How did you know I should have been calling the women?"

"Who do you think headed up the charity ball ticket sales year after year? Who do you think worked the phones for the Junior League fundraisers? Vivi, I know every stuffed wallet in town. I can tell you who will contribute and exactly how much they are willing to part with. As did my mother and her mother before her."

"Why don't I know all this?"

"Because by the time you would have been learning the ropes, I could see that you wouldn't be living your life as Mrs. Somebody Rich. You were meant to be an integral part of Heiser Steel, so we groomed you for that instead." She looked at Vivienne shrewdly. "Not that there was anything wrong with being Mrs. Miguel Abonce. So how are things going in that department? These days his car is parked beside yours more nights than not."

"It's going. We're actually getting along. We're enjoying one another's company with no expectations for anything further."

"Really? Why not?"

"Because we don't love each other. Maybe if we had we could have made the marriage work despite our differences."

"You know how I feel about that."

"And you know how I feel. Unless I love the man and he loves me, I will not be making any more trips down the aisle."

"Oh, child, what am I going to do with you?"

"Put me together a consortium to save the Durango?"

"I'll do my best." Betsy glanced down at the menu. "And in the meantime, we can order some of those greasy tacos your father loved so much."

Chapter Ten

"Jesus, Cameron, I *told* you I answered that email. Three days ago. Why are you bugging me about it?" Vivienne scowled across the room at her brother.

"All right, all right. You answered it. Sorry. I forgot." Cameron collapsed into his desk chair. "I didn't mean to upset you."

Vivienne sighed. "No, Cam, I'm the one who needs to apologize. You didn't do anything wrong." She put her head in her hands. "I feel like it's all crashing down on me. The show closes in two weeks and we still don't have enough to buy out the theater."

"So how is Mom doing at the fundraising?"

"She's good. Really good. But twenty million's a lot of money. It's going to take her more time than we have."

"The clock's ticking. I can hear it in my head." Cameron ran his hands down the sides of his face.

"Do the men know? Have they said anything?"

"They can tell something's going on. I can't help but wonder how much longer they're going to stay."

"Probably until the bitter end. They can't make the kind of money we pay them anywhere else, and they know it." She glanced over at the door that led to the factory floor. "They're the best in the business. Which is why we pay them what we do. Hell, Cameron. Maybe I should have given up weeks ago and told Miguel to get the ball rolling on a sale. The thought of having to let them go nauseates me."

"No," Cameron said sharply. "The Durango's worth something, too." He looked her over with a critical eye. "This is eating you alive. How much sleep did you get last night?"

She waved her hand around her face. "Clearly, not enough."

"Do I have to tell Miguel to go home and let you get some sleep?"

"I sleep better when he's there." She rubbed her temples. "I haven't seen too much of him the last few days. He had some big project he needed to work on. He texted me last night that he was almost finished with it."

Cameron murmured something. He got up abruptly and walked out for a few minutes, returning with a relieved expression on his face before going back out to the factory floor. She turned back to her desk and tried to concentrate, but as the afternoon wore on the headache she'd fought all day began to ratchet up, and it was all she could do not to snap at the shop foreman when he came in with a legitimate question. She was about to give up and go home when Miguel came through the door dressed in work clothes and steel-toed boots. He looked down at her with concern on his face. "*Querida*, you don't look so good."

She shut her eyes and shook her head. "Thanks. Exactly what every woman wants to hear."

"I learned many things during our marriage. Tact wasn't one of them. So how much longer before you can shake loose?"

"Give me ten minutes to shut down. Do you want to meet somewhere for dinner?"

"I have a better idea. Why don't I put you in my car, we'll go out somewhere on this side of town, and I'll bring you back for your car later."

"Whatever." She didn't see why she couldn't follow him wherever, but her head hurt too much to argue.

She answered a couple more emails, returned a phone call, then shut down her computer and followed Miguel out to his company truck. "No time to go home and switch cars?"

"Something like that." He pulled out of the parking lot and headed down the street. Vivienne shut her eyes and rubbed her forehead. "Headache?" he asked.

"A bad one."

"Maybe I have the cure for that."

"What? A hammer to my head?" She shut her eyes against the glaring sunlight.

"Nothing that drastic." He swung onto the access road and got on the expressway.

They were halfway out of town before Vivienne realized how far they had driven. "I thought you said we were eating somewhere close."

Miguel grinned. "Oh, come on. Seventy miles isn't that far. Not really."

"Seventy miles? Miguel, you have to be kidding. What are you up to?"

"I'm kidnapping you for a couple of days."

"But—I—I—I have stuff I need to take care of. I can't possibly leave right now. What about my car? Besides, the theater."

"Will be there when we get back on Friday," he interrupted smoothly. "As will Heiser Steel and all the problems we're leaving behind for the next couple of days. And your car will be fine. Your Aunt Katie will take your mother over to drive it home." He reached across the console and took her hand. "Cameron called me. He and your mom are worried about you. I'm worried about you. You've had three bad headaches in the last week and you're driving yourself crazy worrying about the theater and the company, neither of which you can do anything about in the next few days."

"What about your business?"

"I finished today about noon and spent most of the afternoon clearing the calendar so I could run off with you. On a Tuesday. Which explains my urbane appearance and the work truck. I barely had time to throw a few things in a duffle and pick up your weekender from your mother."

"You and the truck are fine. I hope Mom packed me some stuff I can use."

"If not, Fredericksburg is full of shops."

Fredericksburg? Vivienne felt her objections melt like a snowflake on a hot sidewalk. She loved the picturesque little Hill Country town that had capitalized on its German heritage and its lovely stone houses. "All right. If you insist."

His smile turned into a knowing smirk. "I thought you might say that."

"Where are we staying?"

"In an old Sunday House close to downtown that's now a guesthouse. We can walk downtown and to the museums. Either cook there or eat out and enjoy some of that wonderful German food. And I hear the bluebonnets are spectacular along the highway. It will be light until we get there so we can see them."

They slipped into a comfortable silence. Miguel coped patiently with the snarled traffic leading from the city to the numerous subdivisions that had sprung up the last few years along I-10. Gradually the traffic thinned as cedar trees and cattle-dotted pastures replaced the cookie-cutter subdivisions. Vivienne took in the fields of bluebonnets and other brightly blooming roadside flowers blanketing the grassy median and right of way and spreading over the fenced pastures. She sighed inwardly. Between Heiser Steel and her obligations at the Durango, it had been several years since she'd gone for a ride in the Hill Country during bluebonnet season. She glanced over at Miguel and wondered how long it had been since he'd taken a drive in the Hill Country for anything other than visiting a job site.

She sat quietly and savored the beauty of a Texas spring, the knots in her neck loosening and the tension in her head easing as they sped along the highway. The flowers were thicker and prettier once they'd turned off the interstate onto the state highway leading into the historic little town. "Oh, look. A pasture full of baby goats. They're so cute." The little ones were playing with one another while their mothers munched on grass.

"You see cute. I see *cabrito*," Miguel teased, earning himself a glare.

The sun was dipping low in the sky when he pulled up to a charming little stone Sunday House off Main Street. Fredericksburg had a number of Sunday Houses, mostly built in the late 1800s by farm families to use on weekend trips into town. Many were now guesthouses or bed and breakfasts. Miguel unlocked the toolbox and withdrew two duffle bags and a reusable grocery bag. "Your mom put together some bedtime snacks for us until we can get to the store."

Vivienne peeked into the sack. Chips, crackers, a can of her favorite cheese spread, a small box of bakery donuts, a couple of inexpensive wines in unbreakable cartons, and a box of Keurig pods. Yep, enough to hold them until they could find a grocery store.

Vivi followed Miguel up the steps and watched while he keyed in a code on the electronic lock. "*Listo*," he said as he pushed open the door. "Home sweet home for the next three days." The tiny, one-bedroom cottage was simple, but comfortably furnished with vintage golden oak and an inviting sofa and chair in the living room. The bedroom had a queen-sized brass bed and was covered with an exquisite Little Dutch Girl quilt.

"I love it," she breathed.

"I thought you might."

Miguel threw his duffle bag and her weekender on the bed. Vivienne peeked inside the bag and was relieved to find exactly what she would need for the next several days, including a couple of nicer blouses to wear in the evening. "You want to go downtown for some schnitzel?" she asked.

"Love to. But I need a shower first." He waggled his eyebrows. "We could save time if we showered together."

"Riiight." She shucked her skirt and blouse and threw them on the floor. Her bra and panties followed. Miguel had to sit down on the side of the bed to unlace his boots. The rest of his clothes ended up on top of them in a messy pile, and together they trooped to the tiny but well-appointed bathroom. She eyed the narrow shower dubiously. "You think the two of us will fit in there?"

"Won't know until we try. And we can always stand really close." He pulled her to him and held her tightly against his naked body, his surging desire hard against her stomach.

"Like this close?" She looped her arms around his shoulders. "Kiss me, Miguel. Kiss me and make love to me in that little shower."

"I'm all over it."

They were plastered together from head to toe, his lips fused on hers, her arms tight around his neck, her fingers in his hair. His arms were bands of steel around her waist, crushing her to him as the hair on his chest tickled her puckered nipples digging into his chest. His hard cock thrust into the juncture at her thighs. He pushed his leg between hers, forcing her open so that he could tease her with the tip of his cock. The touch of his lips on hers and the feel of his body so close awakened every nerve ending in her body, hot chills igniting her everywhere they touched.

They kissed for a while. Vivienne inhaled the steel and sawdust scent clinging to his hair and his skin, and the essence that was simply Miguel.

When they climbed into the tiny shower, they squirmed around a bit until they both fit, and then lathered up big loofahs with the expensive body wash provided. Miguel's touch was gentle as he ran the loofah down her body between her breasts. "We used to do this all the time," he said as the loofah dipped lower. "And then we didn't."

"I know." She used her loofah on his muscular chest. "There were lots of things we did until we didn't." Her fingers were deft as they explored his lower stomach. "We should have kept doing them."

"You mean things like this?" He dropped the loofah and snaked his fingers between her legs. Her loofah also hit the floor as she grasped his cock in her soapy hands.

"And this?" His finger found her sensitive nub and touched it the way she loved for him to. She pumped his cock up and down, feeling it grow impossibly harder in her hands.

They intensified their efforts and Vivienne exploded first, a hard orgasm taking her by surprise as she came against his fingers. Miguel followed a moment later, his cock pulsing jets against her fingers as he groaned against her neck. They kissed long and lingering before they picked up the loofahs and proceeded to bathe one another as best they could in the tight quarters.

"Remember that huge shower stall in the resort in Cancun where we spent our honeymoon?" she asked as he squirted shampoo into her hair. "We could have had an orgy in there."

"Sorry for the tight quarters tonight." He grinned mischievously.

"You're not a bit sorry and you know it." She moaned as he massaged the shampoo into her hair.

"What can I say? A beautiful woman mere inches from me? I'm supposed to complain about that?" He aimed the spray down into her soapy hair. "I love your hair."

He'd been saying stuff like that a lot over the past few weeks. She didn't remember him be so complimentary before.

They dressed casually in jeans, T-shirts and sandals, and walked through the balmy night to a café on Main Street featuring German food and craft beer. Miguel opted for schnitzel and kraut and she ordered her favorite, bratwurst and cabbage, accompanied by German-style dark beer and warm rye bread.

The last of her cares melted away as they shared intimate, meaningful looks, the longing in his eyes a promise that their interlude in the shower was only the beginning of a night to remember.

They would have two more days to do whatever they wanted. She knew it wasn't going to last forever. On Friday they would have to pack up and return to San Antonio, to the decision they had facing them and the ramifications of whatever they decided. But she had tonight and two more days.

Her and Miguel in a moment out of time, and she was going to savor it.

***

The next morning, Miguel stood patiently, a smile teasing the corners of his lips as Vivienne pawed through a pile of crafted handmade quilts. She was quite the shopper, he thought with amusement as she zeroed in on a quilt with little girls wearing bonnets. She said something about it being like the one on the bed in the Sunday House and how much she liked it. He filed away a mental picture of the pattern so he could give it to her for her birthday. And they would be together when her birthday rolled around in October. His lips firmed in determination. He'd make damned sure of it.

He wasn't going to let Vivi go a second time.

She finished with the pile of quilts. "See anything else you like in here?" he asked.

Her glance flickered around the small store carrying high-end bedding and linens. "No. I'm not in the market for this kind of stuff. Not these days." Her expression was rueful as she glanced at the big-ticket linens. "It's okay. The ones I bought at Walmart are nice."

Nice? Not for the first time, Miguel admired her attitude toward her new, and hopefully temporary, financial reality. According to her brother, she'd geared down her expectations after the divorce without whine or a whimper. And in all fairness, she hadn't run up huge bills when they were married. She'd lived well with him, but not to the excess that she could have. He wished he'd appreciated that quality in her before. He could certainly appreciate it now.

"So are you done in here?"

She nodded. They continued their meander down Main Street, stopping at a candy store for the fudge he loved and at probably the best kitchen store he'd ever been in. He sprang for a couple of new top-of-the-line knives for his mother and Vivi bought Betsy and Katie a bag of gourmet coffee beans. Vivi window-shopped a couple of mid-price boutiques, but moved on quickly. They lunched on burgers and a wonderful craft beer and were strolling Main Street when Vivienne pointed out an old three-story structure on the corner. "Ever been in there?" she asked.

"Can't say that I have. What is it?"

"The old Nimitz Hotel turned museum. Chester Nimitz was the Pacific Fleet Commander during World War Two. A hero to his hometown." Her eyes lit up. "You want to go inside? I love museums."

"You do?"

She looked at him strangely. "I always have. Doesn't matter what kind of museum. I'll go to anything from masterpiece art works to a tractor museum." He raised an brow and she laughed. "Yep, I've been to one of those. You want to do this one? It ought to be good."

Miguel nodded, hoping his surprise wasn't evident. He'd been with Vivi for five years and was married to her for three and didn't know she loved museums. Except for a couple of society fundraisers, he'd never taken her to a museum, and to his knowledge she'd never visited one without him during their time together.

It made him wonder what else he didn't know about her.

Their first stop was the old hotel and the exhibits about the life of Admiral Nimitz. Vivi studied the displays with interest, taking her time and making the occasional astute observation. They passed through a courtyard displaying the names and pictures of World War II veterans and Miguel promised himself he'd look into having his grandfather's name and picture added.

The next building over was a history of World War II in the Pacific. The exhibits and artifacts were interesting and educational, but he found himself studying Vivienne more than the museum. Her eyes were bright and her expression animated at every exhibit. And she was positively vibrating with excitement as she viewed the Japanese midget sub, the B-25 bomber, and the Japanese float plane. She seemed as excited about the smaller artifacts on display, like the faded uniforms, the Japanese stopwatch, and the old ukulele one of the admirals carried with him.

"It's amazing the way they've brought the era alive," she enthused as they exited the building. "It's one of the best World War Two museums I've ever been in."

"You've gone to a lot of them?"

"A few."

They walked toward an indoor-outdoor exhibit a couple of blocks away. "Why didn't I know any of this? We were together for five years and I had no idea."

"When did we ever have time for museums? You worked all the time and I had Heiser Steel and the theater." She looked over at him. "I bet there's a lot I don't know about you. What's something that you love, or used to love, to do that I don't know about?"

He thought a minute. "I love going through houses."

"I know that. You make a lot of your living renovating them."

"No. I mean I love going on house tours. Old mansions. Historic houses. Houses famous people lived in. Parade of Homes. Builder demo houses. Frank Lloyd Wright houses. Craftsman homes. The Newport Mansions and the Biltmore are at the top of my bucket list."

"I didn't know that about you. Never would have expected it. What else do you like to do?"

"I used to own a Harley. I used to love to take it for a spin on Twisted Sisters. That's—"

"I know about Twisted Sisters. One of my boyfriends in high school used to take me up there in his Corvette. We loved those wicked curves. What happened to the Harley?"

"I sold it when I got too busy to ride it."

"That's too bad. I'd love to ride on the back of a Harley sometime."

"So you like twisting roads and killer curves?"

She nodded and looked at him wistfully. "We could have gone riding. I like old houses too. We could have gone to some houses together. I would have enjoyed doing that with you."

"As you said, we didn't have time for that kind of thing."

"No, we didn't make time for things like that. We didn't have that kind of marriage." She scuffed at a clump of grass with the toe of her tennis shoe.

"We blew it, you mean."

"Yep, we did."

They were silent as they went through the Pacific combat zone exhibits and the Japanese Garden of Peace. Miguel was beginning to realize that they made a lot of mistakes during their marriage.

Maybe their union hadn't been the stuff of romantic fantasies, but they should have spent time together. They should have gotten to know one another as people and not only sexual partners. They should have gone places together. He should have taken her to museums. She should have gone with him on house tours. He should have bought another Harley and taken her riding. They should have spent more time and energy on their relationship and less on their careers and the Durango. They should have worked a little harder on their marriage.

Miguel straightened his shoulders with resolve. They would do better the next time. At least he would, and he hoped from her comments this afternoon that she would, too.

Because there was going to be a next time.

Even if Vivi didn't know it yet.

***

Vivienne stared out at the horizon from the top of Enchanted Rock, her breath stolen by the majestic view from the enormous pink granite uplift north of Fredericksburg. The Hill Country spread out for miles in every direction, the limestone hills covered with cedar and grass and a sea of blue and red and yellow flowers. Fredericksburg could be seen to the south. She wasn't sure, but she thought she could see the little town of Llano to the north. "Kind of takes your breath away," she said as she gazed toward the hills in the distance.

"In more ways than one." A wheezing Miguel handed her a bottle of water from his backpack. "I thought I was in shape." He opened another water and drank deeply. "You never even breathed hard."

"It's the dancing. I couldn't have done it that easily before I got in shape for *Anything Goes*."

"Then I don't feel so bad." He wiped his brow with the hem of his T-shirt, exposing his stomach and most of his chest and earning himself a whistle from an older hiker dressed in hippy gear and a sun bonnet.

Vivienne raised her brow and looked the older woman in the eye. "He's taken."

The woman smiled impudently. "Figured that. But nothing to stop me from admiring the view up here."

"You have a point." Vivienne grinned and winked.

The woman ambled off and Miguel sat on the large boulder next to Vivi. A warm breeze lifted the hair off Vivienne's temples. "So I'm taken, huh?" Miguel asked as they sipped their water.

Vivienne started to make a snappy comeback. But she glanced over at him and the look on his face froze the words in her mouth. He wasn't kidding. He really wanted to know where he stood with her. "I don't know."

"It's a simple question, Vivi."

"No, it isn't. And you know it." She looked out at the sprawling vista and collected her thoughts. "We went into this with no expectations. The deal was to table our debate over selling the Durango and enjoy one another's company for the duration of the run."

"At which time we would revisit whether or not to sell. We've already had that discussion." He took her hand. "I know nothing's settled, but at least we're not fighting about it anymore."

"Which is something."

He rubbed his thumb over her hand. "Tell me, have you had fun these past few weeks?"

"You know I have." She turned to him, knowing he could see that she was troubled. "But it... we are different. We managed to resurrect everything that was good about our relationship. Are you ready to jack that?"

"What if I want more?"

What if I want it all? What if I want to love and be loved? Vivienne bit her lip. He said he wanted more, but he said nothing about love. He didn't love her. He never had, and never would.

Which cut through her like a knife. The pain took her breath away. To live with him and care for him, and even marry him again, knowing he didn't love her. She wasn't sure she could live with that for the rest of her life.

"What more do you want, Miguel?"

It was his turn to hesitate. "I don't exactly know. But I've enjoyed being with you again."

"Likewise."

"And I don't want it to end."

She didn't either. But if she stayed with Miguel in a loveless relationship, she would never find the kind of love she was looking for.

She finished off her water. "Tell you what. We enjoy the rest of our getaway. We finish the play, and we deal with the Durango and Heiser Steel. Then, we'll see where we stand at that point." She squeezed his hand. "You take the time to think about what you want and so will I."

Miguel didn't look pleased. "So let me reiterate. Am I taken, Vivi?"

She placed a gentle kiss on his lips. "We'll talk about that later."

They followed the trail down to the base. Miguel's good humor seemed to be restored by the time they reached the parking lot. They drove back into town, and after another sexy shower—it was amazing how creative they could be when tightly confined—they spent the rest of the afternoon visiting a few of the numerous art galleries that were sprinkled through town.

They had their usual argument over sleek and modern versus traditional and romantic, and Miguel ended up buying her an impressionist-style courthouse painting and taking home a stark black and white cityscape photograph for himself.

The sun was setting in the western sky as they sipped wine on the outdoor patio of an old stone house that had been converted into a high-end steak place. "Thank you for a lovely getaway," she said as she swirled the rich red cabernet. "It was wonderful."

Miguel looked across the table at her. "It doesn't have to end, Vivi. At least not quite yet. And, we still have tonight."

She nodded. "We still have tonight."

They savored their steaks and wine. Miguel drove them back to the Sunday House where they spent hours in one another's arms. They curled up together, exhausted, and for the time being, sated. Miguel fell asleep quickly, his breath warm against the back of Vivienne's neck. She lay still, her body relaxed in his arms, but her mind in a whirl as she pondered their discussion.

She wasn't surprised he didn't want it to end. Neither did she. They'd managed to put aside the bones of contention that had destroyed their marriage and, with fewer expectations, established a relationship that was working. If they could sell the Durango to the consortium, the last roadblock to a successful relationship would be gone.

But, as lovely as the last few weeks had been, they weren't what she longed for in her heart. Miguel had never once told her he loved her. And she didn't love him.

Or did she?

She eased out of his arms and turned over, studying his face in the moonlight filtering in through the gauzy curtains. He looked younger in sleep, without the cynical shrewdness in his eyes and the tightness around his mouth. Vivienne reached out and touched his cheek, steeling herself from the unwelcome and unwanted emotion that threatened to take her breath away.

Shit. She'd gone and done it. She'd fallen in love with him. She'd dropped her guard, and sometime in the last two months he'd sneaked past her defenses and found his way inside her heart.

She felt tears gather. Foolish. Unbelievably foolish. She'd given her heart to a man who didn't love her. He wanted what they had before, minus the fights and the friction. That was more than enough for him.

It wasn't enough for her and never would be.

Damn her traitorous heart.

Chapter Eleven

Miguel watched as Vivi stood in the theater's wings listening to the thundering applause as the band played and the cast members strode to the edge of the stage to take their final bows. The already deafening applause grew louder as first the ensemble appeared, then the angels, the ship's captain and crew, and the other supporting characters.

Finally the other leads came out in pairs according to their role. The audience rose to their feet when Wade and Jessica appeared, the applause overwhelming for the two young actors.

And then it was Vivienne's turn. She ran to the footlights, smiling and curtsying and blowing kisses to the crowd. Miguel didn't know how the audience could get any more enthusiastic, but the noise level ratcheted up yet another notch as the closing night audience let Vivi know how much they'd enjoyed her performance.

Pride swelled in his chest as he watched her graciously accept the roses offered to her by her brother, and the accolades that were her due on this last night of the show.

The actors basked in the adulation, then the stage lights went on and the curtain came down. The cast took their places in the lobby to greet their audience and accept their compliments.

Under Letti's direction, Miguel and the rest of the crew began striking the set. Letti had told them that the ocean liner would be taken apart by the set designer and the pieces either re-used or otherwise recycled in future productions.

The actors returned to the dressing rooms where the costume designer was waiting with a checklist for each actor of items to be returned. The mood was festive as the actors took off their costumes for the last time.

The cast drifted, most of them headed to the cast party Letti was hosting. Miguel and Vivienne had hosted a couple during their marriage, but when their relationship soured Cameron had taken over the reins. But since Cameron had given up his spacious Alamo Heights midcentury modern for a smaller cost-friendly condo, he could no longer host the event.

The crew gave the backstage area a thorough clean. Miguel was about to leave when Letti called the crew together. Puzzled, he watched as she handed an envelope to each of them. "Your honorarium," she said when he raised his brow.

"You didn't have to. I wasn't expecting anything," he protested.

Letti gave him a half smile. "You earned it same as any other crew member. You did a great job. Thanks."

"You're more than welcome." He pocketed the envelope, not sure what to do with it. They could put the money to better use than paying him.

"You're coming to the cast party, right? I busted my ass all morning to get the house clean."

"I'd love to. Thanks for the invite."

He hadn't been expecting that. The attitude of the cast and crew had mellowed over the weeks of the show, especially when it became common knowledge that he and Vivi were seeing one another, and that he was working with her to save the theater.

He pulled out his phone and Letti added her contact information. "Do I need to bring anything?" he offered.

"We have the food covered. I wouldn't say no to a couple of six-packs."

Miguel swung by a convenience store and picked up a couple of chilled six packs of Corona. His GPS took him to a house a few blocks away from his mother and grandmother's home. There were cars parked on either side of the street for a good block in either direction. He parked and made his way toward the house.

The party sounded like it was in full swing when Miguel rang the bell. Letti's daughter Sophie answered the door. "Come on in. Mom has a cooler in the kitchen for the beer and wine. Margarita pitchers are on the kitchen counter, and food's on the dining room table."

He made his way through the crowded living room, pausing every couple of feet as the cast and crew stopped him to say hello. He finally found the kitchen, where Vivienne and a couple of cast members were putting out party trays and mixing a fresh pitcher of margaritas. He unloaded all but one of the beer bottles into the cooler and opened the last one. One of the girls eyed his beer. "I would have thought you'd be more of an expensive Scotch type."

"Nah. Where I grew up, this was the big treat. That and rotgut tequila if we were really feeling frisky. How about you?"

"A New Orleans Sazerac if I can get it. Otherwise, a sweet wine."

"Blech. I don't know how you can gag those sweet things down." Vivienne made a face.

"You like beer?" the girl asked.

"No, Vivi is a Pinot Grigio kind of girl. Or Sauvignon. The drier the better."

The girl shuddered and headed for the dining room with a party tray.

Miguel peered over Vivi's shoulder. "Can I do anything to help?"

"We have it under control. Go mingle and have fun." She made a shooing motion.

"If you say so."

The living room and family room were packed with cast and crew and a slew of significant others, so he headed for the less populated patio, where he found Josh and Wade and a girl Miguel had not met sitting at a picnic table enjoying the spectacular sunset. They motioned him over and introduced him to Maggie Gutierrez. "Maggie's our fundraising guru. She writes our grants and secures donations," Wade explained.

"Delighted to meet you," Miguel said as he shook the girl's hand.

"The pleasure is mine," she replied warmly. Miguel groaned inwardly. If he'd known about Maggie, maybe she could have helped them assemble the consortium.

"Are you glad it's over?" Josh asked him with a smile.

"Yeah, but it was more fun than I thought it would be." He took a pull of his beer. "When would be a good time to have you and Cameron sign the affidavit?"

"Anytime you want. Tomorrow morning, if it works for you. You'll need to ask Cameron what works for him." He glanced around and lowered his voice. "Vivi told us all about the plan to sell the Durango to a consortium, but she's concerned that you can't raise enough money. How's that coming?"

Miguel took a breath. "It's coming. Not as fast as I hoped, but Mrs. Heiser has worked the phones for the last two weeks and the lady knows what she's doing when it comes to getting blood from a turnip. I've made a few calls too. Some of my old friends have done well. You may be seeing some new faces at the Academy. I used it as a selling point."

"We'd welcome the kids. You know that," Maggie enthused.

"We're doing our best, Josh," Miguel reassured him.

"We appreciate that. Cameron admitted their company's about to go under. We don't want that to happen, either," Josh said.

"Yeah. Heiser Steel's been in that family for five generations and the trouble it's in started long before Cameron and Vivi took over."

"I was surprised when I heard how bad it was," Maggie said. "From what we've seen here at the theater, Cameron's got a good head for business."

"Have you reached out to the Harrington family or the Navarros yet?" Wade asked. "If you haven't, you ought to. I know they're loaded."

"Amen to that," Maggie murmured.

"And how would you two know this?" Miguel asked.

Maggie smiled crookedly. "My sister married into the Navarro family. Believe me, they're loaded."

Wade grinned wickedly. "Mom's married to a Harrington grandson and his sister's one of my best friends. He and Mom bought a vineyard with his trust fund. Paid cash for it. Here, I think I have a card somewhere."

Wade fished around in his wallet and handed Miguel a card. He thanked Wade and stuffed the card in his pocket. They tossed around a few more prominent names for Betsy to approach before Miguel wandered back inside. He finished his beer, loaded a plate with party food, and spent the next hour and a half having several more discussions along the lines of the one he'd had with Wade and Josh.

Despite his cautionary caveats, the Durango crowd was firmly convinced their theater would be saved and almost tearfully grateful. He hoped like hell he and Vivi hadn't gotten everyone's hopes up for nothing. The bottom line was that they needed to sell the property for enough for Vivi to have the money to bail out Heiser Steel.

Miguel hadn't talked to Betsy in almost a week and had no idea how much the pot had grown. And he'd shut down discussion of the topic with Vivi. He'd be damned if she got any more stress headaches on his watch.

But he hoped like hell that when he sat down with the Heiser family tomorrow afternoon, the news would be good.

***

Vivienne pulled up the latest tax assessment for the Durango Street Theater and whistled under her breath. The downtown property assessments had come out and everything on Cesar Chavez from Interstate 37 to Interstate 35 had gone up in value between twenty-five and forty percent. The value of the Durango had risen thirty percent since last year's valuation. She shut her eyes and breathed in and out. If they sold the property to a developer or someone else willing to pay top dollar, she and Miguel would make out like bandits, and in one fell swoop she would be able to get Heiser Steel back on its feet. Joe's debt to Miguel would be almost paid in full.

And the Durango Street Theatre would be history.

If they sold to the consortium, the theater would be saved. But she was afraid that her half of the money wouldn't be enough to save Heiser Steel. She was under strict instructions from both Miguel and Betsy not to get daily updates on the funds raised, and to put it out of her mind until the show was over.

Yeah, right. She wasn't supposed to worry about the theater she loved or the company that had been in her family for five generations, or the fact that she'd foolishly fallen in love with a man who never would return her love. But she'd tried to put it all out of her head as they'd asked, and had managed to keep the banging headaches at bay.

Now the show was over and the day of reckoning had arrived. Josh and Cameron had signed their affidavits and as of noon today the Durango Street Theatre and the building next door officially belonged to her and Miguel.

Her mother and Miguel were meeting Vivi and Cameron at the office and she and Miguel would hash out the best course of action, based on the funds her mother had raised. While the final decision would be hers and Miguel's, they felt they owed Cameron the courtesy of hearing his opinion, even if they didn't act on it.

She looked down at her hands on the keyboard and willed them to stop trembling.

She made printouts of the Durango tax assessment and was working up a bid for a construction project south of town when Cameron came through the door carrying the fated sack of tacos. "I know you said you didn't want anything, but you need to get something in your stomach even if you have to hold your nose to make yourself swallow."

"Please. It's not that bad. What did you bring?"

"Oh, some *tripas* and *lengua*." When she gagged at the thought of eating intestines and tongue, Cameron barked out, "Jeez, Vivi, I'm kidding. I got us weak-stomached gringos good old *carne guisada*."

"That's not funny." She glared at him and yanked the sack from his hands. "I used to hate it when Miguel would eat that crap in front of me."

"Been eating any of those Mexican delicacies in front of you lately?"

She handed Cam two tacos and took a third for herself. "No. These days he sticks to gringo-friendly fare around me."

"So how's it going? I thought you'd be clawing his eyes out by now, and instead y'all took back up with one another."

Vivienne sighed and bit into her taco. "It's going. We went into it with no expectations and it took a lot of the pressure off. I have no idea where things will go from here." She took another bite of her taco.

Cameron eyed her thoughtfully. "And that's all you're going to tell me, isn't it?"

"Pretty much." She and Cam were close in some ways, but she wasn't in the habit of discussing her love life with him. Besides, she could hardly tell Cameron how she felt when she didn't know herself. "So how's Barry? Are you still seeing him?" She didn't much like Cameron's current boyfriend, but she took comfort in the fact that Cam changed boyfriends on a regular basis.

"Kind of. Not as hot and heavy as it was in the beginning." *Thank goodness.* "And that's all I intend to say about that."

"Fair enough."

Despite her nerves, she managed to finish the oversized taco. She tried to work on the bid, but as two o'clock drew nearer, her concentration dropped to completely distracted. Instead of the words and numbers in front of her, she had visions of standing in the footlights as she had last night, bowing to a full house clapping, stomping, and whistling while she smiled and blew them kisses.

She imagined walking through the Academy with Jessica, watching the six-year-olds singing "Do Re Mi," and Sophie Aldrete tap-dancing to *Anything Goes* in front of a wall of mirrors.

Vivi saw her own face in that mirror as she fitted the prosthetic nose and applied the god-awful green goo that transformed her into the Wicked Witch of the West, while Sandra and Noelle stood beside her turning into Dorothy and the Head Munchkin.

Memories flooded Vivi's mind like a spinning kaleidoscope of moments both special and mundane at the Durango. She looked up at the ceiling and breathed in and out, terrified that after today, all she would have of the Durango Street Theatre would be those memories.

Miguel walked in her office at exactly two. Given his attire, he'd come straight from a construction site. His face was solemn and Vivienne felt her heart drop to her toes. "The news is bad, isn't it?"

"I don't know." He dusted off his backside and sat down in a rolling chair. "I haven't talked to your mother in almost a week."

"You haven't?"

He shook his head. "Bugging her every day would have been counterproductive. She's doing the best job she can and I didn't want to make her feel pressured."

"Thank you for that."

The front door opened and Betsy strode in carrying one of Tripp's old briefcases. "Hello, everybody," she said cheerfully with a big smile. "Where do you want me to sit?"

Miguel vacated his chair and pulled it up to the conference table. Vivienne hoped her mother's smile was a portent of good news, but she couldn't be sure. Unless pouting about not getting her way to go on overpriced cruises, Betsy was perpetually cheerful.

Vivienne called Cameron while Miguel arranged more chairs around the conference table. Cameron popped in right away and the four of them sat down.

Betsy opened her briefcase and removed four stapled documents, handing one to each of them and taking the fourth for herself. Vivienne passed around the printouts of the Durango tax assessment. The room was silent for the next few minutes as they went through the documents. Vivienne was fighting back tears as she raised her head. "Mom raised about two-thirds of the newly assessed value of the property. My half wouldn't save Heiser Steel, and Miguel's half won't cover what Uncle Joe owed him."

Betsy's face fell. "I did the best I could, Vivi. I'm sorry it's not enough."

"Mom, you did great. You raised over ten million dollars from over seventy-five investors. That's phenomenal by anyone's standards," Vivienne said quickly.

"That's right, Mom. You did wonderfully," Cameron was swift to add. "If it had been property anywhere else in town, it would have been more than enough."

"If the property had been anywhere else in town, we wouldn't have been in this quandary in the first place," Vivienne said bitterly. "What is it they say about real estate? Location. Location. Location." She leaned over and took her mother's hand. "It always was a long shot." She sniffed and turned to Miguel. "I guess you better call Horace Foster back and see if he's still interested." She fought back tears as she looked at the three of them. "With Heiser Steel gone, I couldn't afford to keep the theater anyway."

Miguel looked down at the paperwork thoughtfully. "Before I make that phone call, there's another option we—you and I, Vivi— might want to consider."

"What option is that?" she asked quietly.

Miguel raised his head and looked Vivienne in the eye. "We sell to the consortium and use my half to buy into Heiser Steel."

Vivienne took a sharp breath. Miguel was wearing his negotiating face. He wanted something in exchange. "So what do you get in return? Besides partial ownership of Heiser Steel."

"We remarry."

"*What?*" She was sure she'd heard him wrong. "You want me to marry you again?"

"You have to be fucking kidding me," Cameron exploded. "She has no business marrying you to save the damned company."

"Oh, really?" Miguel asked calmly. "That's not so different from why we married the first time, Cameron. Then it was my cold hard cash for the Heiser family social standing and business connections. This time it's my cold hard cash for the company." He turned to Vivienne. "And you have to admit that the last couple of months have been pretty damned fun. We're good together, Vivi. We could make a go of it this time around."

"But—but you don't love me." Vivienne felt her heart pounding in her chest. "You never have."

"You don't love me either."

Vivienne flinched inwardly. She did love him. But she'd be damned if she admitted it, especially after he'd agreed he didn't love her. "Did it ever occur to you that maybe that's why our marriage failed? That we don't love each other?"

"Not really." Miguel shrugged. "We like each other well enough, and we've learned to get along, and the sex is great. Seems to me that ought to be enough."

"Miguel, please," she snapped, mortified. "Not in front of Mom."

"Oh, Mom doesn't mind a bit." Betsy laughed. "He can talk about great sex all he wants."

"Well, I sure as hell mind," Cameron snapped. "Heiser Steel's belonged to the family, and only to the family, for five generations. I don't want outsiders buying in. If we'd wanted that, we would have made a public offering a long time ago."

Vivienne could feel herself start to hyperventilate. "I promised myself I wouldn't do it again. I wouldn't marry for money. I'd only marry if I loved the man and he loved me."

Miguel's lips thinned. "That's ridiculous and you know it. You and I can offer one another things that are a whole lot more important than love." He turned to Cameron. "And I can't believe you'd turn down the offer out of pride. Pride you can't afford."

"Hear, hear." Betsy stood up and put her hands on her hips. "I've heard enough. It's my turn to talk." She turned first to Cameron. "Cameron, darling, your objection to Miguel buying into Heiser Steel is ludicrous. Not wanting it to go out of the family? If Miguel marries Vivienne again, it will most certainly be in the family because *he* will be family. I hate to break it to you, son, but the next generation of Heisers will be Aboncés."

Cameron's lips tightened and his face turned a dull shade of red. "Whatever."

Vivienne blinked as her mother turned to her. "Sweetie, you know how I feel about this falling in love business. It may be fun when you're sixteen, but that's not why you marry a man. What Miguel has offered you is a hell of a lot better foundation for a marriage than love. Yes, the two of you blew it before, but you and Miguel have both said you've learned to get along, and apparently have some other entertaining things in common besides his money and your pedigree. If you get my drift."

"I get your drift." Vivienne felt her face turning red at her mother's frank assessment of their relationship.

Betsy's face softened. "Besides, even if you don't love Miguel, you love that theater with a passion. This way you get to keep the theater. You get to keep Heiser Steel. And you go back to a man who can offer you a hell of a lot. Tell me the truth. Has your life been all that wonderful since your divorce?"

"No."

"Mine hasn't been all that great either," Miguel said quietly. "That condo's damned lonely. I miss you, Vivi. I want you back."

"Screaming fights and all?"

"There won't be screaming fights this time. I get where you're coming from with the theater. I won't complain about it anymore."

Vivienne's thoughts tumbled around in her head. Betsy had nailed it. Miguel's offer would make it possible to save the Durango, rescue Heiser Steel, and enjoy the lifestyle she'd taken for granted most of her life. She should be jumping for joy.

But what about love? a little voice in her head kept asking.

Maybe love wasn't in the cards for her. Maybe she should tell that little voice to shut the fuck up and take what she was being offered. She could do a hell of a lot worse than being Miguel's wife again.

She nodded slowly. "Okay, then. I marry Miguel and the consortium buys the Durango, and he buys into Heiser Steel."

"And they all lived happily ever after," Cameron deadpanned.

"Would you rather lose Heiser Steel and have to go to work for somebody else's company?" Betsy snapped.

"Fine. I'll dance at their wedding." Cameron raised his hands in defeat.

They spent an hour nailing down the details. A visibly ticked-off Cameron returned to the factory. Miguel called his lawyer and arranged for him to take care of the consortium paperwork as well as Miguel's buy-in to Heiser Steel.

They scheduled a meeting for the following week to sign all the papers. Betsy began planning the wedding with gusto. "Simpler than the first one, of course. But a wedding nevertheless." Then she rushed out the door to get started.

And Vivienne sat at her desk and wondered what she had just agreed to.

Chapter Twelve

Vivienne parked in Wade's driveway next to his gigantic pickup truck and knocked on the front door. The sun had set a few minutes ago and the pleasant middle-class neighborhood was bathed in twilight's glow. The day had been almost hot, but the air was cooling, and by the time the rest of the Durango crowd arrived, the evening would be perfect for the patio party Wade and Jessica had arranged in Vivienne and Miguel's honor.

The theater's office staff had sent up a jubilant cheer when she'd telephoned them with the news that the Durango would go to the consortium, and Jessica had called the next morning with news of tonight's get-together. "It's not like we really need an excuse to party," her friend had laughed. "But saving the theater? That's real cause for celebration."

So was saving Heiser Steel. Vivienne and Cameron had called the employees together the next afternoon and reassured them that the company would once again be on sound footing. She had introduced Miguel as new part owner and he'd assured them that she and Cameron would still be in charge of the business. They had served cake and sodas and introduced Miguel to most of their employees, whose big smiles and relieved expressions let on how worried they must have been, and how happy they were that the business wasn't going under.

She had not mentioned her remarriage to Miguel, but the big ring on her finger told its own story.

In one fell swoop, she had saved the Durango and Heiser Steel. Both her beloved theater and her family's livelihood were in good shape and would continue to be.

So why wasn't she happy?

As she raised her hand to knock again, she glanced down at the new ring. She and Miguel had picked it out yesterday afternoon at the most exclusive jeweler in town. She still had her ring from their first marriage, but Miguel insisted on getting her another. "A new ring for a fresh start." He'd gifted her with something completely different from the first one: an oval solitaire, simpler and less ornate than its predecessor, but still obviously expensive.

Maybe he hoped that a different ring would mean their marriage would also be different. She sure hoped so. Especially since she was doing the one thing she'd said she wouldn't, marrying a man who didn't love her.

Once again, she was marrying for money and lust.

And to the same man.

But it wasn't the same, she told herself as she knocked again on Wade's door. This time she loved Miguel. Maybe her love for him would be enough to hold them together.

Wade looked sheepish as he pulled open the door. His hair was wet and he wore only a pair of jeans. "I laid down for a nap and woke up five minutes ago. I just took the shortest shower on record. Come on in."

"I brought a tray of vegetables to put on the burgers and some chips and gourmet dip from the fancy grocery store. You can bring them in for me when you get your shoes on."

She followed Wade inside and he disappeared down the hall. From the lack of clutter and general air of emptiness, she gathered that Wade was living alone these days. A couple of pieces of furniture were missing. Noelle's basket of toys no longer sat in the corner, and Sandra's pictures no longer graced the bookshelves. Vivienne had always wondered exactly what Wade and Sandra were to one another. They always claimed to be roommates and nothing more. But whatever they had been, Sandra was home in Tennessee with her no-longer-estranged husband, and it was clear that Wade missed both her and her delightful little girl.

Wade returned dressed in a T-shirt and flip-flops. "Most of the regulars will be here tonight. The RSVP emails came in yesterday and today."

"That doesn't surprise me. This bunch likes to party. We'd celebrate a clipped hangnail."

"And this is some serious reason to celebrate." They trooped out to her car. "I didn't get an email from Cameron. Did you hear from him?"

"I doubt he's coming. He's... it's a long story. I'll tell you later." She'd be damned if she admitted to Wade that her brother was being pissy. He had barely spoken to her since the decision to sell part of Heiser Steel, and had said flat-out that nothing about the deal she'd made with Miguel was worthy of celebration.

Wade and Vivienne were unloading the food from her car when Jessica parked at the curb. She unbuckled her son from his car seat and the child made a beeline for Wade, who hugged the little boy and put him on his broad shoulders. Jessica smiled as she unloaded a small cooler from her trunk. "Looks like Bobby found his best friend," she said as Wade managed to balance the child with one hand and carry a grocery sack with the other.

"This is my best buddy," Wade said as Bobby held onto his curly hair. "Ouch, little man, don't pull." He ducked down enough to get through the front door with the child on his shoulders.

Jessica stared after them wistfully. "Bobby asked me the other day why he didn't have a daddy like the rest of the kids. He wasn't too impressed when I told him his daddy's in heaven." She looked down and spotted the ring on Vivienne's hand. "My God, when did this happen? I thought you were only hanging out."

Before Vivienne could answer, Letti and Rachel pulled up. "I'll tell you about it later," Vivienne murmured.

It wasn't long before the party was in full swing. The men manned Wade's massive grill while the women laid out munchies and fixings on the kitchen table and breakfast bar. Letti kept the margarita pitcher full and Josh and Hector kept the cooler stocked with beer and sodas. Miguel came in with a case of his beloved Corona and more triple sec and tequila for the margaritas.

The first batch of burgers was about to come off the grill when Josh let go with a sharp whistle. The partiers quieted down and he motioned Vivienne and Miguel to the patio. "I'm not going to talk long. But I want to thank these two wonderful people for saving the Durango. Miguel Abonce and Vivienne Heiser, you two are the best ever. So let's give them both a rousing cheer."

The group went into a chorus of "Hip, hip, hooray," and "Speech." Miguel clasped Vivienne's hand and raised it and everyone quieted. "I'm not talking long either," Miguel said. "But I do want everyone to know that Vivienne has done me the honor of agreeing to once again be my wife. Thanks, Vivi." He leaned over and gave her a hard, swift kiss on the lips that had the blood rushing to her head.

The crowd cheered again, although some of her closer friends, like Jessica and Wade, looked puzzled. But their congratulations seemed sincere as they assembled the burgers and dished up the rest of their meals. She sat down at Wade's big picnic table and Miguel slid in beside her a moment later. "They're really happy about the theater," he observed as he bit into his burger.

"Of course we are." Jessica had Bobby by the hand and was balancing a plate of food in the other. She sat Bobby across from Vivienne and plunked the plate down in front of him. "Bobby can eat first. I'll eat later."

"Not necessary," Miguel said. "Sit him over here beside me. I'll watch him while you get your plate."

Vivienne wasn't sure who was more surprised, Jessica or Vivienne. But maybe she shouldn't have been. Miguel had a nephew about Bobby's age that he doted on. And he'd not argued when Betsy said the next generation of Heisers would be Abonces. Maybe he wanted a child with her this time around.

The thought made Vivienne uneasy—bringing a child into a marriage that wasn't based on love. On the other hand, Miguel's children would be beautiful and he would love them, even if he didn't love her. And she would love a child of Miguel's with all her heart.

Miguel managed to keep Bobby entertained until Jessica returned, bringing a couple of the ensemble dancers with her. The mood was mellow as they ate and drank and laughed and celebrated saving the Durango. The dusky lilac of twilight slowly faded into the inky blackness of a moonless night, with only a sprinkle of stars visible in the night sky. Bobby was starting to nod off, so Jessica took him into the house. The ensemble dancers excused themselves and wandered off. Miguel leaned over and brushed her lips with his. "I've got to go, *querida*. I have a breakfast meeting in the morning at seven. I'll see you tomorrow night."

She murmured her farewell and Miguel disappeared. The party had mostly drifted into the family room, leaving her by herself on the patio, which suited her mood perfectly. As lovely as the party had been, she didn't feel all that celebratory. Which was ridiculous.

She had managed to pull it off. She had saved both the Durango and Heiser Steel. She should be floating on air.

Jessica came back outside a few minutes later. "I put him down in Noelle's old room. He's out like a light."

"I guess he still misses his pal."

"He does. Although they talk on Skype pretty often."

"How's Noelle?"

"Absolutely thriving. And you should see Sandra. She's glowing. Happier than I've ever seen her. She and that little hillbilly must really love each other. Oh, and she went back to her old nickname. She goes by Cassie these days."

"To me she'll always be Sandra." Vivienne took a deep breath. "So she and her husband really love each other. Must be nice."

She could feel Jessica's eyes on her in the dark. "Scary comment coming from a woman who's sporting a new rock on her left hand. What brought that on?"

"Why'd you marry Robby?"

"I loved him. I loved him practically from the first time I laid eyes on him. I was a senior in high school and he was one of the young cops who came to Career Day. He gave me the once-over and I slipped him my phone number. The rest was history. Way too short of a history. I've been a widow longer than I was a wife. Why did you ask?"

"Just wondered."

"Come on, Vivi. I know you better than that. Why did you ask me why I married Robby?"

Vivienne sighed. "Because, for the second time, I'm about to marry a man who doesn't love me. There goes my dream of happily ever after with a man who does."

"*What?* You don't love Miguel? And he doesn't love you?"

"I didn't the first time I married him. He didn't love me then, and he doesn't love me now."

"So why get married to him again? For that matter, why marry him in the first place?"

"We married the first time because he wanted entrée into the inner circles of San Antonio society. Businessmen who wouldn't look twice at a scrappy businessman from the barrio were more than happy to do business with Tripp Heiser's son-in-law. In exchange, he kept me in the nice things I couldn't pay for anymore. Oh, and the sex was off the charts."

"Lust and money."

"Pretty much. And it wasn't enough. We fought over the theater and his working long hours, and it finally got to be too much."

"So why are you marrying him this time?"

"It was the deal we struck to save the theater and Heiser Steel. We sell the theater to the consortium for way less than it's worth and Miguel puts his half of the profits into Heiser Steel for a percentage of the company. And in exchange I marry him again."

"Lust and money round two?"

"I'm hoping there will be more things going for us this time around. Amazingly, we seem to have learned to get along and have fun together. We go places and do things as a couple that we didn't before. Like that getaway in Fredericksburg. We had a ball up there. We never did stuff like that when we were married. Maybe this time around we will."

Jessica looked at her. "He may care more about you than you think. Especially if there's more to the relationship than sex and money."

"Nah. We've only added fun to the equation."

"I'm sorry, Vivienne. I'm having trouble wrapping my head around that. But I'm not the one who matters. It's you. Are you going to be all right with this? Marrying a man you don't love?"

"I never said I don't love him."

"Does he know?"

"No, and I'm not about to tell him. The last thing he wants is my love."

"Is it going to be enough? Your loving him and knowing he doesn't feel the same way?"

"I guess it will have to be. Besides, who knows? Maybe I was never going to find that love anyway."

"And maybe you have and you just don't know it."

Vivienne looked at Jessica. "Would that you are right about that. But somehow I don't think so."

***

Miguel flipped over on his back and put his hands behind his head. It was late, he was tired, and he had to be up at the crack of dawn. But his thoughts kept spinning like a hamster on a wheel. He should be the smuggest, most satisfied man in San Antonio. It had been a huge financial sacrifice, but he'd managed to convince the woman he wanted by his side to give marriage to him another go. His ring was on Vivi's finger, and her mother was planning a wedding. He should be on top of the world.

Instead, he was plagued by doubts.

He was beginning to wonder if they were doing the right thing getting married again, or about to make the most colossal mistake of their lives.

He hadn't missed the look on Vivi's face tonight when he announced their engagement. She should have looked happy. Or at least pleased. Instead, she had a deer-in-the-headlights expression on her face.

He kept drifting back to the meeting with her mother and brother when he'd offered to marry her again. She hadn't been exactly inspired. She'd insisted she wanted to marry for love and only agreed to marry him after he and Betsy laid out his case. He'd hoped Vivi would get past her reluctance and show the same enthusiasm for this marriage as she had their first one. Not so. If anything, her uneasiness seemed to be growing.

He'd thought she'd be happier being married to him again. This time around, they would have all the good things they'd shared without the friction. They would have fun. They would have great sex. He would buy her anything she wanted. Heiser Steel would thrive and she would continue to entertain the people of San Antonio on the stage at the Durango.

He thought she would be thrilled.

***

Vivienne smiled at Josh and Rachel across a restaurant table overlooking San Antonio's Riverwalk. "This was supposed to be a quick meeting in your office. How did we end up eating lunch on the river?"

"We all showed up an hour earlier than we had to and heard Riverwalk calling our name," Rachel teased.

"More like we finished up our business in record time and smelled the barbeque," Josh stated.

Vivienne laughed. "Whatever. This hits the spot." She took another bite out of her messy brisket sandwich. "I love it down here." A barge full of enthusiastic tourists glided by, passing beneath the arching footbridge and disappearing around a curve.

"Why don't you and Miguel buy a condo in one of the new buildings? That way you could enjoy it all the time."

"He already has a lovely condo close to his offices. We lived there when we were married before." And if they ever had a child, a downtown condo wasn't the place to rear one. But she didn't voice the thought. She and Miguel hadn't yet broached the topic of children this time around and she had no idea whether he wanted them.

Come to think of it, there were a lot of things she didn't know regarding this upcoming marriage.

A marriage she was beginning to feel like was a noose being lowered around her neck.

"Only a thought," Rachel said cheerfully.

"And a good one," Vivienne assured her.

"Speaking of thoughts, what would you think of us doing *How to Succeed in Business* either later this year or early next year?" Josh asked. "Cool or too retro?"

Rachel rolled her eyes. "Josh, there is no such thing as too retro. People love those old musicals."

"I second that," Vivienne said. "Can't you see Wade as J. Pierpont Finch?"

Josh made a kissing motion with his lips. "I can see that sexilicious dude playing about any role he wants."

"Down, boy," Vivienne teased. "Don't you have a main squeeze at home?"

Josh grinned unrepentantly. "I'm not supposed to touch; doesn't mean I can't look." He grinned. "Anyway, do I look into getting us *How to Succeed*?"

"I say go for it. Unless you have any other plays you're thinking about," Vivienne said.

They tossed around ideas until their plates were empty. Josh and Rachel's excitement was palpable. Which was why Vivienne was marrying Miguel, she reminded herself as they divided up the bill.

Rachel and Josh headed back to the Durango. Vivienne wasn't due at Eloy Solomon's office until two, so she sat a few minutes watching the tourists and locals stream up and down the sidewalks and over the bridges. She soaked in the ambiance and tried to shut her mind to the doubts that were growing stronger about her upcoming marriage to Miguel.

She had been convinced marrying a man who didn't love her was the wrong thing to do the first time around. Why the hell do it again?

She didn't have a plan B.

She couldn't bear the thought of losing the theater and disappointing the people who treasured the Durango as much as she did. And she had no intention of losing Heiser Steel.

Fuck it. She'd do what she had to do.

Besides, what she had with Miguel wasn't bad.

It wasn't love. But it wasn't bad.

Vivienne put the top down on the Beamer and drove ten miles above the speed limit all the way to Eloy Solomon's office. Miguel's car was in the parking lot along with another set of high-dollar wheels she figured belonged to the consortium chairman.

Miguel's attorney had set a speed record drawing up the paperwork for the consortium, and Betsy had wheedled Tripp's old friend Byron Summerset, whose son Kevin had done a few shows at the Durango, to serve as chairman.

As Vivienne got out of the car, another vehicle pulled up and she recognized J.D. Felding, the owner of the biggest construction company in the city. She stared at him for a moment and wondered what he was doing at Eloy Solomon's office this afternoon. Only one way to find out.

The pink-haired receptionist ushered Vivienne into the conference room where Miguel waited with Byron Summerset. Byron was in the middle of a story about his son's latest exploits in Hollywood when Eloy walked in with J.D. Felding and a man Vivienne didn't recognize. Eloy looked as surprised to see Byron as they did to see his companions. Eloy introduced Felding and his attorney and Vivienne introduced Byron. "Mr. Summerset is here in his capacity as the chairman of our consortium."

"What consortium?" Eloy asked.

"The consortium that's buying the theater," Miguel said. "My attorney should have contacted you by now to inform you that we assembled a consortium and that we would be selling the theater to them."

"Oh, dear." Eloy look a little green. "I apologize for not getting back to you on that. I've been out of town at a family funeral and flew in this morning. I haven't had a chance to even check my email." Eloy motioned for Felding and his companion to have a seat. "I wish I'd gotten your message. I could have saved you the trouble of bringing Mr. Summerset this afternoon." Eloy looked across the table at Vivienne and Miguel. "I'm also sorry you went to the trouble of assembling a consortium to sell the theater when the theater's already been sold."

"*What?*" Vivienne snapped. Red-hot rage made her dizzy, and she turned to Miguel. "What's this about it already being sold?"

"I don't know," he ground out. He turned to Eloy. "Would you care to explain?"

Eloy sighed. "Joe got a fantastic offer on the property days before he died. He talked to me about taking the offer but he wanted the two of you to work a show together. He had the notion that maybe you'd get back together or something. After he accepted the offer, he gave me strict instructions not to say a word to you about the sale until his plan played out. We drew up a codicil reflecting the sale and that the profits would go to the two of you once you'd both worked the show." He handed everyone a copy of the codicil and the paperwork from the sale.

Vivienne read through the documents, every word a knife slice to her heart. The codicil spelled out that the property was sold and that she and Miguel were to split the considerable proceeds. Felding's company was to take possession of the property fourteen days after Vivienne and Miguel signed off on the sale.

She wasn't an attorney, but she'd read enough contracts to know this one seemed to be in order and that fighting it would probably be pointless. The Durango and the adjacent building now belonged to Felding Enterprises to do with what they wished.

The Durango Street Theatre was history.

The codicil was signed and dated three days before the last performance of *The Wizard of Oz*. Three days before Miguel had scoped out the theater.

She felt the tears burn behind her eyes as she turned to Eloy. "You should have said something," she snapped. "We made fools of ourselves for nothing." She wiped her cheeks. "Damn it. Why would Uncle Joe do this to me? He knew I loved the Durango."

"If I'd known you were trying to put together a consortium, I would have headed you off," Eloy told them quietly. "Neither of you said anything to me."

"Per your instructions, well, Joe's instructions, we thought it would be ours to do with as we saw fit. Who knew it was a goddamn farce?" Miguel's voice trembled, his face mottled with fury.

"And as to why he did what he did, I believe that ring on your finger pretty well answers that question," Eloy added gently.

"The Durango's gone. Nothing else matters now." She drew in a deep breath. "Give me the paperwork. I'm sure Mr. Felding can hardly wait to put his bulldozers to work."

Eloy pushed the papers across the table. "You're the pink tabs. Mr. Abonce is the green."

She scrawled her name on all the pages with pink tabs and handed the papers to Miguel. Tears fell and dotted the table as he signed his name beneath hers and then gave the paperwork back to Eloy. "Are we finished here?" she asked dully.

"Your part is finished, yes," Eloy answered.

"Then I'll not take up any more of your time." Wiping the tears from her face, she stood and swept from the room.

She was almost to the front door when she felt a gentle hand on her elbow. "I'm so sorry," Byron murmured. "I hate like a son of a bitch what happened in there."

"What I don't understand is why Joe didn't leave us the money. Miguel's right. Why the farce?"

"Only Joe knows the answer to that."

"Do you think the consortium would be willing to purchase another property?"

"Is there another property out there to buy?" he asked. "Let me rephrase that. Is there another property that the consortium members are willing to buy? Half of them were interested only because it was the Durango. Some thought it was historic, and others have memories of going to the movies there when they were a kid. I don't know if they'd be willing to buy something in a suburban strip mall. I'm sorry, Vivienne."

"So am I, Byron."

She was almost to her car when Miguel slammed out of the building. His eyes were narrowed and his features tense. Vivienne slumped. She didn't have the energy for this right now.

She waited until he stopped two feet in front of her. "Vivi, you have to believe that I didn't know a thing about what Joe did. Why would I have offered to buy into Heiser Steel or let your mother spend all that time putting the consortium together?"

"I know. You looked like you were ready to kick an embolism in there. No one's that good an actor." She looked down at the ring on her hand. "You made me an offer to save the theater and my company. The theater doesn't exist anymore, and the price of marrying a man who doesn't love me is one I'm not willing to pay."

For a moment, he looked like she'd shot him through the heart with a sawed-off shotgun. Then he straightened. "You don't love me, either, Vivi. Marriage is like any other business arrangement. It's all about assets, *querida*. Who is bringing what to the table."

"You know what? I just lost the thing in this life that I love with all my heart and you're standing here giving me a Wharton Business School lecture. I don't want a business deal. I want a husband I love who loves me back. I deserve that much out of life and I'm going to get it." She pulled the ring off her finger and pushed it into his hand.

He turned away and walked to his car. Her hands trembled as she beeped open her car. She heard him pull out of the parking lot as she slid into her seat. As she started the engine and got the air conditioner going, fat, sloppy tears ran down her cheeks.

"Why, Uncle Joe?" she whispered. "Why did you sell it out from under me? We could have saved it."

Chapter Thirteen

Vivienne stood on the sidewalk outside the Durango and watched as Wade's loaded pickup truck, and the last of the U-Haul trucks, with Maggie behind the wheel, pulled away from the curb. "Was that everything?" she rasped as Josh and Cam came out of the building. They were hot and tired, and covered with dust and grime.

"Everything that isn't nailed down or tied on." Josh rubbed his hand down his weary face. "The Felding lackey said some kind of salvage company is coming this afternoon to take down a couple of light fixtures and the neon signs in the lobby." He glanced back at the theater. "There's not a whole lot in there that would be desirable as resale. It's not retro enough."

"If it had been all that retro, the historical society would have stepped in and helped us save it," Cameron said. "Problem is, it isn't old enough or fancy enough or unique enough for them to bother. If it had only been ten years older."

"But it wasn't, and it will be gone by five this afternoon." Vivienne didn't try to hide her bitterness. "Has Rachel or Miranda called you?"

Rachel and Miranda were at the storage facility they were renting to store what they had taken out of the theater over the last two weeks. Josh and the women—on the payroll until the end of the day today—had spent the last week triaging everything from pianos to popcorn machines. The more valuable items, like the sound equipment and speakers and microphones and such, were going to a climate-controlled facility. The sturdier stuff was being stored in various garages. Letti and Wade had both filled half their two-car garages with Durango boxes and Jessica had let them fill her attic. It broke Vivienne's heart to leave the curtains, but Josh pointed out that they had been at the point of replacing them anyway.

Besides, curtains were useless if you didn't have a stage to hang them on.

"Rachel said there would be room for everything, but that it would be a tight fit."

They looked at one another. "I guess this is it," she said as she looked at Cameron and Josh.

"You're not coming back this afternoon?" Josh asked softly.

Vivienne closed her eyes. "Yep. Sucker for punishment that I am. You?"

He nodded.

"Cam?" Her brother glanced at her and it was all she could do not to cry. He looked as gutted as she felt. "I guess so. If you two can watch it come down, so can I. Come on. Let's go find something to eat."

"I'm not hungry." Vivienne sighed.

"You need to eat, Vivi," Cameron said firmly.

"Besides, I'm starving," Josh said. "You can watch us eat."

They walked a couple of blocks to a popular hamburger joint. The little place was full and had a half-hour wait for a table, so they ordered their burgers to go and agreed to sit on a bench in Market Square to eat them.

"How goes the job hunt?" Vivienne asked Josh.

"Truthfully, I've been so down in the dumps I haven't done anything yet. I'll have time next week to polish up my résumé and send it out. In the meantime, there's always a place for me at Goldstein's selling dress pants. The family would love for me to quit this theater nonsense, as Bubbe would say." Josh's family owned one of the better men's apparel shops in town and his grandmother campaigned constantly for her only grandson to become part of the business. "I keep telling her that selling isn't my thing, but she's not one to take no for an answer."

"At least she's not pressuring you to go to med school," Vivienne teased. "I'm not so worried about you. Or Rachel. Your bubbe will give you a job as long as you need one and Rachel can wait tables at her uncle's restaurant. It's Maggie and Miranda I'm worried about."

"Miranda said she has some savings," Josh said. "You don't need to worry about Maggie. She said her father had work lined up for her next week."

"Oh, shit," Vivienne and Cameron said in unison.

"What?" Josh asked.

"Never mind. What you don't know won't hurt you." Cameron's tone said, *And don't ask again.*

Their burgers arrived and they moved to a bench where they spent the next few minutes eating. The men polished theirs off, but Vivienne put hers down after eating only half. Cameron picked up her unfinished burger and gobbled it up.

"So what happens now with the consortium?" Josh asked.

"It's unraveling as we speak," Vivienne stated. "Mr. Summerset nailed it. The only reason people wanted to save the Durango was because they have fond memories from their childhoods. They aren't willing to buy any old place. Not that there seem to be any old theaters lying around. The one place for sale that could be remodeled into a theater is on the edge of King William and is worth at least as much as the Durango, if not a little more. And the historical society has their claws so deep in it, there wouldn't be any remodeling it anyway." Her hand fisted on the table. "The whole thing is so fucking unfair."

"What does Miguel think about it?" Josh asked.

"I don't know. I haven't spoken to him since I gave his ring back."

"Yeah, I noticed the rock was gone. I thought maybe you took it off to work."

"No, she gave it back, as well she should." Cameron squeezed her hand. "Josh, he doesn't love her. He cut a business deal: sell the theater to the consortium, and buy into Heiser Steel if she would marry him again. He wants her for her social connections."

"Kind of like the first time," Josh said.

"Right," Cam replied. "I'm glad she didn't do it. She needs to find man who cares for her and not what she can do for him."

"Really? Sounds to me like he cared about you, Vivienne, if he was willing to give you both the theater and save your company," Josh countered slowly.

"Nope. I was another asset." She swallowed the lump in her throat. She'd be damned if she cried in front of Cameron and Josh.

Their mood was somber as they trudged back up the street to the theater. A small crowd had gathered, familiar faces that all shared the same desolate expression. Rachel and Miranda were standing together. Jessica and Maggie each had Wade by the hand. Almost the entire casts of *The Wizard of Oz* and *Anything Goes* were there.

Two television stations and the newspaper had reporters and photographers present.

One of the television reporters spotted Josh and Cameron and made her way through the crowd to them. "Would either of you in your official positions with the theater care to comment on what's happening today?"

Josh and Cameron both made polite statements of regret that a city treasure was being lost. Then the reporter zeroed in on Vivienne. "Ms. Heiser, you and Miguel Abonce of Abonce Construction Company were named as co-owners of the building. Do you feel you could have done more to save it?"

It was all Vivienne could do not to throttle the reporter. "The theater was sold prior to Mr. Lang's death. Mr. Abonce and I were left the profits, not the theater."

"But isn't it true that you used your share of the proceeds to prop up your family's faltering company rather than save the theater?"

"As I said, the theater was *already sold.* Mr. Abonce and I never took possession of the property. There was a plan in place to save the theater, but we were unable to implement it because the theater was ALREADY SOLD. Believe me, if I could have saved the theater, I would have."

The reporter, perhaps taken aback by Vivienne's vehemence, thanked her and moved on to interview other Durango supporters.

Across the street, a small group of men wearing hardhats and shirts with Felding logos stood conferring. Two men and a woman in white coveralls were carrying out the largest neon sign from the lobby. A bulldozer was sitting in the street and a crane with a wrecking ball attached was in the space behind the theater. Traffic was being rerouted around the dozer and police were preparing to block the street entirely. Vivienne wondered for the umpteenth time why Felding had chosen such an inconvenient time to do the demolition. Maximum publicity, she guessed. The company had wasted no time announcing their plans to build a twelve-story building housing doctors' offices and an outpatient clinic. A worthy project that could have been built somewhere else.

The workers stowed the neon sign in a van and drove off. The police began cordoning off the street. Vivienne pointed to the marquee. "They're going to bulldoze the sign? They *can't.*" Before anyone could stop her, she ran across the street, Cameron at her heels, to the group wearing the Felding shirts. "Who's in charge? I need to speak to whoever's in charge here."

To her surprise, J.D. Felding himself stepped forward. "That would be me. How are you, Ms. Heiser?" He looked at her impassively.

She swallowed back a lump in her throat. "Could you please take a few minutes and remove the marquee before you demolish the building? It would mean so much to me... to us. I'll gladly pay you for it."

She felt Cameron's hand on her shoulder. "We would consider it a tremendous favor."

One of the other men spoke up. "Mr. Felding, we don't have time. The permit is only for a two-hour window."

Felding started to shake his head. "Please," Vivienne pled, cursing that she had to beg for something that should have been hers.

Felding looked at them and across the street, where the Durango crowd stood solemnly watching, and the TV cameras were rolling. "We can spare fifteen minutes to get the lady her sign." He looked at her with a hint of compassion. "You don't have to pay anything. It was going to be demolished."

The objecting minion barked something into his cell phone. Vivienne looked at Felding with tears in her eyes. "Thank you."

Felding nodded once. Cameron pulled out his phone and by the time the workers had removed the marquee, Wade's truck was by the curb. Thankfully he was well stocked with moving blankets, rope and bungee cords. It took four men to take down the marquee and strap it to Wade's massive truck. He did a U-turn and pulled into the parking lot across the street.

Vivienne clutched Cameron's hand as the crane engine and bulldozer roared to life. She watched in fascinated horror as the wrecking ball smashed into the Academy building. Two hits, four, five, and the small, cheaply built building was rubble. Then the crane operator swung the wrecking ball and hit the Durango directly where the marquee had hung. She choked back a sob as the building seemed to absorb the impact. But the second hit left a huge jagged hole in the second story wall. The ground shook with each hit, as chunk by chunk the Durango's walls and roof hit the ground. Bigger, and better built than the first building, it took hit after hit. But before long, it too was down.

Tears streamed down Vivienne's face as she looked at the ruins. It was gone. Despite her best efforts and the efforts of those around her, they hadn't saved it. It was lost to her forever. She would never audition for a part there again. She would never put on a costume or do her makeup or strap on a mic in the dressing room again. She would never sing or dance or act on its stage. She would never shake hands in the lobby or encourage a young dancer or do any of the things Vivienne loved doing at the Durango. It was all over.

A heartbroken sob escaped, and then another, and before she could get a grip on her emotions she was crying helplessly into Cameron's shirt, her brother's arms little comfort as she mourned her loss. He held her tightly and murmured comforting words in her ear and she could feel his tears in her hair. "I'm sorry, Vivi," he murmured over and over. "I'm so damned sorry."

She cried for long moments before she could get herself under control. She raised her head and found her friends watching her solemnly, most of them with tears in their eyes also. There was a round of sad hugs. One by one, the heartbroken crowd drifted apart. Wade said he'd found a place to store the marquee and drove off with it. When the last of the theater people had departed, she got in her car and drove away.

***

Vivienne's tears had dried up by the time she got to her condo. She poured herself a big glass of wine and sank down onto the sofa. The story would make the news tonight. She wondered what spin the media would put on it. She had no doubt that she and Cameron would be prominently featured in the story. And she had no doubt she would find her picture in the business section of tomorrow's newspaper.

She wondered if they would include Miguel's name and picture, too. Probably. Most likely, he wouldn't appreciate having his name linked with hers, now that the engagement was off.

Vivienne steeled herself as a fresh stab of pain sliced into her midsection. She knew she had done the right thing breaking it off. The marriage was bound to fail. And she couldn't be expected to be the only one in love in the relationship. But as she stared out the front window, she wondered if her sense of loss over the Durango would be so profound if Miguel was beside her.

How much of her devastation was over the loss of the theater, and how much of it was over the loss of Miguel?

***

Miguel sat with his feet on the windowsill and stared blankly out the fifth-story window of the old bank building across from the Durango, or what had been the Durango. The sun was low in the western sky, casting an orange-red glow on the pile of rubble that had this morning been the Durango Street Theatre. The last of the theater supporters had dispersed hours ago, as had most of the Felding company's people, leaving only a few of Felding's employees along with the bulldozer and its operator, who spent most of the afternoon shoveling debris into a series of industrial dumpsters lined up on the sidewalk.

Nighttime work lights had been positioned an hour ago, and from the speed the cleanup was going, the lot would be cleared by morning. He looked down at the Scotch bottle sitting on the desk in the unused office he'd borrowed for the afternoon. He'd only had one shot and that was hours ago. It was perfectly safe for him to get in his car and drive home. But he couldn't seem to tear himself away from the window. Instead he watched as the love of Vivi's life was shoveled off the ground and into commercial dumpsters.

Would that she loved him like she had that old theater.

He'd watched her as she talked to the reporter, her eyes flashing with anger at something the reporter asked. He'd watched as she ran across the street to plead her case for the old marquee and the heartbreak on her face as Wade and the Felding workers strapped it to Wade's truck. It had just about killed him to watch her flinch every time the wrecking ball slammed into the old building. It was all he could do to keep himself from running down and taking her into *his* arms when she broke down and sobbed in her brother's.

He longed to hold her.

Not that she would want him to.

Miguel sighed and hauled himself up. Staring out the window wasn't going to bring Vivi's beloved theater back to life. And it wasn't going to bring Vivi back into his life. *Dios*, he'd come so close to having her back. She had agreed to marry him again and had his ring on her finger. And then everything had blown to hell in the lawyer's office. There was no saving the theater, and she had the money to save Heiser Steel without his help.

He'd wondered more than once if things would have been different that afternoon if he'd told her how he felt instead of talking about business arrangements and assets. Maybe if he'd handled it differently, she would still be wearing his ring.

Probably not. It wouldn't have mattered. She didn't need him anymore.

He picked up the Scotch and carried it down to his car. He wished things had gone differently. If they had, he could have been her knight in shining armor and saved the theater.

He missed her. He missed everything about her. Sleeping by her side, drinking his morning coffee with her, rubbing her tired shoulders, and her rubbing his. Her sleepy smile first thing in the morning. He missed the possibility of her having his children and spending their lives raising them and spoiling grandchildren together. He missed the idea of growing old with her and holding her hand someday when that was about all they could manage.

Miguel swore as he pushed the button and his car's engine sprang to life. The irony of his situation wasn't lost on him. He was the one who had scoffed at the thought of marrying for love. He was the one who insisted marriage was little more than a business deal. He was the one who'd denigrated Vivi's dream of loving and being loved in return.

And now he was damned.

He had fallen in love with a woman who dreamed of love with anyone but him.

*****

Miguel pulled into Eloy Solomon's parking lot and climbed out of the work truck. He was between job sites and was hot, dirty, and aggravated. This afternoon he had yet one more hoop to jump through to get his money from the sale of the Durango. The Feldings could have done an electronic funds transfer or sent his check by courier. Hell, they could have even put it in the mail. But no, they had insisted he waste part of his afternoon picking it up and signing for it in person. That he had to go back to Eloy Solomon's office to do it was torture. Miguel was still furious with the attorney for not leveling with them in the first place. He'd had his lawyer go over the will and the codicil. Despite Solomon's supposed promise to Joe Lang, there was nothing in writing that would have prevented the attorney from telling the truth from the get-go. He wouldn't have worked the show. Vivienne would have performed knowing that the fate of the Durango was a done deal. Vivienne and Cameron wouldn't have had to worry about Heiser Steel. Miguel and Vivienne would not have gotten involved again.

They both would have been spared a lot of grief.

He would not have fallen in love with her and gotten his heart broken.

He wouldn't have lost any chance he might have had to win her back someday.

In place of the pink-haired receptionist sat an older woman with a round face and kind eyes. He stated his business and asked for the check. "It's in Mr. Solomon's office and he's in a conference right now and asked not to be disturbed. He shouldn't be that long." She smiled sweetly.

Miguel looked at his watch and swore. "I don't have all day," he ground out. "I'm due at another job site within the hour."

"I'm sure it won't be that long." She smiled even more brightly.

Miguel sat down. He stretched his legs out and crossed his arms in front of him. Ten minutes and he was out of here and they could get him the money some other way. He was done jumping through hoops for Joe Lang and Eloy Solomon.

It was going on nine minutes when Solomon ushered a tearful young woman to the front door. The woman left and the attorney sighed. He walked over to Miguel and shook his hand. "Come on back." He seemed amused by Miguel's impatience.

He shut the door and motioned Miguel to a chair. "Here's the check and the receipt you need to sign." He handed Miguel an envelope with the check showing through the window. He gave him a second piece of paper to sign.

Miguel scrawled his name and handed the paper back to Solomon. "Is this the last damned hoop I have to jump through?"

"I'm sorry you felt like you were jumping through hoops." Solomon looked at him with a smile on his face. "But you have your money and that lovely lady's yours again. So wasn't it all worth it?"

"You have to be kidding. She gave me back my ring before we got off your parking lot." He didn't even try to hide his bitterness. "It might have been different if she'd gotten to keep the theater. But three days ago she watched *her* theater get torn down. She fell apart. She lost the thing she loved the most."

Solomon's smile faded. "I'm sorry. But you kind of lost me."

Miguel almost stood up and left the office. But, what the hell? Eloy Solomon had been all up in their business without them knowing it since before Joe died. What difference did it make now if Miguel laid it out for Solomon?

"We were going to sell the Durango to Byron Summerset's consortium for maybe sixty percent of what it was really worth. In exchange, she was going to marry me and we were going to use the entire proceeds to save Heiser Steel with me assuming a minority percentage of the ownership. It would have been a win-win. But now her theater's gone and she can save Heiser Steel with her share of the profits. She doesn't need me to do it for her." He tossed the pen on the desk. "I don't know what the hell Joe had in mind when he concocted his dumb-ass scheme, especially since the outcome was a foregone conclusion. He managed to hurt me and he hurt her even more. She honestly thought she could save the theater. I honestly thought I could have her back. We both got screwed over."

"Well, hell." Solomon sank down in his chair. "That's the last thing the romantic old fool would have wanted." He sighed. "Joe and Tripp were devastated when you and Vivi divorced. Tripp extracted a deathbed promise that Joe would do whatever he could to get you two back together. Tripp was certain that his daughter and the son of his heart loved one another and had somehow simply lost their way."

"I don't know what Tripp was thinking."

"I don't know either. I do know that when Joe learned that his days were numbered, he concocted the plan. He was sure that by doing a show with Vivienne that you would understand her passion and that the two of you would get back together. He figured the theater would be sold anyway, so he went ahead and accepted Felding's offer. If he'd known you would find a way to save it, he might have done things differently."

"Doesn't matter. The theater is gone and Vivienne's lost to me forever."

"You really think that?"

"Why would she come back to me? The only reason she was willing to remarry me was because she needed me."

Solomon folded his hands in front of him and looked at Miguel sternly. "Then it behooves you to find a way to be needed, doesn't it?"

Chapter Fourteen

Vivienne sat back in her desk chair and tried to be excited as she read the email. They'd landed the contract to supply all the metalwork for the new Emmanuel Bible Church sanctuary. The Hill Country megachurch had outgrown its five-thousand-seat sanctuary and wanted to build one twice as large. It was a substantial contract and would yield a tidy profit and keep their employees busy for months. Cameron would be so happy. He'd been delighted when they'd landed two much smaller jobs earlier in the month. This one was going to knock it out of the park. And now that their debts were dealt with, they were operating in the black, and this new contract would push out their profit margin.

Betsy was already looking for a bigger condo, and if she could find a nice one for Vivienne close by, so much the better.

Not that Vivienne gave a damn about a condo or anything else these days. Sure, she was relieved that creditors were no longer pestering them and that they were landing contracts again. Word spread quickly in the San Antonio business community, and once builders and construction companies knew that Heiser Steel was on solid ground financially, the company's reputation for quality work brought business back to their door.

She was glad the company that had been in the family for five generations would live on for the next generation of Heisers.

That was if there was a next generation of Heisers. At the rate she was going, her biological clock would run down and stop ticking before she had any.

Vivi sighed and clicked on the next email. More than once in the last month she'd been tempted to say to hell with it and call Miguel to see if he still wanted to be with her. But then she remembered the contempt on his face when she'd said she wanted love in her marriage.

She had been wrong to marry him the first time knowing he didn't love her. It would be stupid beyond belief to marry him again knowing he still felt that way. She would keep the love she felt for him to herself and spend her days and her energy on Heiser Steel.

It was the nights that were the problem. No husband to come home to, no rehearsal to rush off to, no lines to learn, no performance to give. Only a book or a movie that couldn't hold her attention while she mourned her losses. The loneliness enveloped her like a scratchy wool blanket.

Vivienne shook off her morose musings and went through her emails. She had reached the last one and was about to start putting together a bid to supply the steel for a new grocery store when Betsy stuck her head in the front door. "I have a couple of hours before I need to get started on my next telephone list. Could I interest you in going somewhere for lunch?"

"Mom, I—"

Her mother stepped into the office. "Cameron said you were down in the dumps and that you could use some cheering up. So will you humor your worried mother and come out for lunch? If we eat enough we don't have to cook dinner."

"You've convinced me. Not having to cook supper sounds good." Vivienne pushed herself out of the chair. "The taco place next door?"

"Nah. Let's be a little more creative than that. I'll drive."

They tossed around restaurant ideas and ended up at a big, barn-like steak house along the expressway. Their waitress met them at the door with salads on a tray and showed them to a small table in the back. The table had a lively red checked tablecloth and a lazy susan with a choice of salad dressings. "I haven't been here in ages," Vivienne murmured as she read the menu, which was a painted sign on the wall. "Not since before Miguel and I started dating. The first time." She sighed. "So get me caught up. Have you and Aunt Katie found a place to live that's more to your liking?"

"Not really. The job is taking up loads of my time and Katie may be moving in with her new boyfriend." Betsy's eyes danced with mirth.

"Her *what*? Since when? I thought she'd sworn off men for good."

"I did, too. But you know Katie. She's unpredictable, if nothing else."

"So how do you like your new job?"

"I love it. According to my supervisor, I have a real gift for talking people out of their money." After her success at raising the money for the now-defunct consortium, her mother had landed a job as a professional fundraiser and was doing a bang-up job of it.

"That's wonderful, Mom." Betsy wasn't making a great deal of money, but she wasn't out thinking of ways to spend it, either.

Their waitress brought them big glasses of tea and took their orders. They both opted for the rib-eye and mashed potatoes. The girl said their steaks would be right out.

"So get me caught up on you," Betsy prompted.

"Heiser Steel is thriving. We've landed several contracts and this morning the company building the new auditorium for that megachurch out on I-thirty-five awarded us that job. Cameron said he's going to have a lot of the guys working overtime."

"Fantastic. How about the other?"

Vivienne raised her eyebrow. "What 'other'?"

"Whatever one you want to tell me about. But I was asking about the acting. Have you approached any of the other theaters in town?"

Vivienne rolled her eyes. "Every single one of them."

"And?"

"And damned little. Three of them are trying to go equity, which knocks me out totally because I don't have equity credentials and have no desire to obtain them. The others said I'd be welcome to audition, but their shows are cast way in advance, which means they won't be holding any auditions for months. One of the directors was honest enough to tell me that while I'm welcome to audition, they already have a talent pool they usually draw on."

Betsy frowned. "I never realized it was like that. I thought new actors were welcome."

"At the Durango they were. But the Durango was one of a kind. Hey, look at me. I managed to say 'Durango' without crying. I'm making progress."

Betsy's smile faded. "I am so damned sorry for the way things turned out. I can't believe Joe let you think the theater was going to be yours."

"Knowing Uncle Joe, it was probably a cockamamie scheme to get me and Miguel back together."

"It almost worked."

"It would have worked if the theater hadn't already been sold." Vivienne doused her salad with a generous dollop of Thousand Island dressing.

"Tell me," Betsy said softly. "Can you say 'Miguel' without tearing up?"

"Yep. That one pinches around my heart."

"Aw, you miss him, sweetie, don't you?"

"Of course I miss him. We were practically inseparable there for a couple of months. That condo's damn lonely with no Miguel and no theater to go to."

Betsy took a deep breath. "I think you should go back to him. He'd take you back in a heartbeat."

"I agreed to marry him again because he offered me a way to save both the theater and the company. The theater's gone and I saved Heiser Steel with my own money." She ran her fork through the salad. "Maybe it's for the best."

"Why would it be for the best? You've admitted you're lonely and that you miss the man. Besides, even if you don't need him anymore, his reasons for wanting to marry you again still stand."

"I know that. You and I have been over this ground before. I did a lot of soul searching after the divorce and even more in the last month. And the more thinking I do, the more I'm convinced that the only valid reason to marry is for love and only for love.

"Miguel and I should never have married in the first place. I was wrong to marry him for his money and I'm not doing that to him, or to myself, again." She held up her hand when her mother started to protest. "I know you insist that you and Daddy married for the same reasons we did. But Mom, I have memories of the two of you together. Daddy had this little smile that was just for you. And you always looked at him like he was your hero, even when he was anything but. Miguel and I never had those kinds of moments when we were married."

"And later? When you were spending time together during the play? I have eyes, too, Vivi. I saw the way you looked at him. There was love in your eyes."

"I guess there was. I was stupid enough to fall in love with him this time. But it means nothing, because he doesn't love me back. He told me flat-out after the fiasco in the lawyer's office that marriage to me was nothing more than a business deal. He said marriage was about who brought what assets to the table. I'm nothing more than a business asset to him, and if the sex is great, so much the better. I want to marry for love, and even if I love him, he sure as hell doesn't love me."

"You're certain of this?'

"You should have seen him scoff at the thought of marrying for love."

"Miguel has been known to scoff when he's feeling out of his depth. He may be a millionaire now, but sometimes that insecure kid pokes his head up." Betsy sipped her tea. "So you think you're another asset to him."

"Pretty much."

Betsy's lips twitched. "An awfully expensive asset, if you ask me. Or not much of an asset at all, if you put a pencil to it."

Vivienne looked at her mother. "Maybe you'd like to clarify that? Since we both know damned well he married me to have access to Daddy's business connections."

"Oh, I'm hardly denying that. And he would have had those again. But think about what it would have cost him. Literally. He would have been out the millions that would have been his share of the Durango sale. He would have been buying a minority share in a company that frankly he never had a bit of interest in. No offense, sweetie, but all the business connections in the world aren't worth that kind of money. Especially now that he's already made those business connections, for the most part."

She reached over and grasped Vivienne's hand. "He would have had to want you back pretty badly to make a financial sacrifice like that. He would have had to really care about you to offer you what he did. Maybe he doesn't have the pretty words to tell you he loves you. Maybe he's afraid to admit he cares. I'm not a shrink. I don't know. But I got to know him pretty well when you were married. Miguel wouldn't make that kind of sacrifice unless he cared a hell of a lot."

"I don't know, Mom. I wish I agreed with you."

"Tell you what. You think on it some. Think back to the man you were married to. And ask yourself why else he'd make that kind of sacrifice for you. Promise me, Vivi."

Vivienne nodded. "I promise."

But she didn't think she would be changing her mind about Miguel any time soon.

***

The steak and Betsy's company had made Vivienne feel better. She tackled the proposal and was deep into calculating the cost of the plate metal that would be needed for the grocery store job when the front door opened. She looked up from the computer screen and the smile on her face froze when Miguel stepped inside and closed the door behind him. He looked at her with solemn eyes. "Hello, Vivi."

She nodded her head in acknowledgement. Her heart pounded in her chest and her hands began to tremble on the keyboard. He was here. The man she loved was standing right in front of her. She hadn't seen him since Eloy Solomon's parking lot. She hadn't heard a word about him. It was as though he'd dropped off the planet.

He had come from a job site. His hair needed a trim, and he had circles under his eyes and lines around his mouth, the way he had when he'd been working too hard. With her and the theater out of the picture, he'd probably gone back to his workaholic ways.

Which made her wonder what he was doing here in the middle of a work day. She tried and failed to give him a smile. "Hello, Miguel. What brings you to our neck of the woods?"

He looked at her with what seemed like uncertainty. "I want you to come with me and look at something."

The door to the factory floor opened and Cameron came through. He pulled off his welding goggles and took off his ear protectors. "I see you made it." He and Miguel shook hands.

Vivienne looked at her brother. "You knew he was coming? You didn't tell me."

"No, I didn't tell you. Miguel called me this morning. He ran something by me that he wants to show you." His face was as solemn as Miguel's. "I think you should go see it."

She looked from her brother to Miguel, mystified. "Would either of you care to tell me what it is that you want me to see?"

"No," they said in unison.

"It's not something I can tell you about," Miguel said. "You need to see it for yourself."

"You know I hate surprises." She didn't try to hide her exasperation.

Cameron put his hand on her shoulder. "Go with him, Vivi. I think you'll be glad you did."

She took a deep breath. "Whatever. I won't get that bid written up until tomorrow."

"Tomorrow's soon enough. Shut down your computer and scoot." Cameron and Miguel exchanged a look.

This went beyond odd. The last time Cam talked about Miguel, he had nothing good to say. Now they were in cahoots?

She shut down the computer. Miguel held the door for her and opened his truck door so she could climb inside. The hot May sun shimmered off the dash and the gravel parking lot. Miguel put down the windows for a moment to let out the hot air and cranked up the AC as high as it would go. He slid his sunglasses on his nose and pulled out onto the street. His face was impassive as he headed toward the expressway, but his hands clutched the steering wheel a little too tightly.

He was nervous about something.

She waited for him to talk, but he remained infuriatingly silent as they passed through downtown. They were on I-10 and she wondered if he was taking her on another out-of-town trek when he took an exit and turned into one of San Antonio's older neighborhoods.

Her curiosity ramped up a notch when he made two more turns that landed them in the middle of the Deco District. The old neighborhood had been built in the twenties and thirties, the same as her neighborhood, Alamo Heights. It was home to a hodgepodge of architectural styles, from English Tudor and craftsman to Spanish colonial and bungalows. An interesting assortment of businesses lined the main drag, and buried in the neighborhood was the beautiful and historic Jefferson High School. Unlike Alamo Heights, which was as chichi as it had ever been, the Deco District had gone into decline after its heyday. But for the last few years it had enjoyed a renaissance, as singles snapped up the bungalows and young couples and families wanting something other than suburban living moved into the larger houses. An interesting part of town, certainly, but not one Vivienne knew all that well. She still couldn't fathom why Miguel would want to show her something over here.

He turned onto the main drag and drove until he pulled up in front of an abandoned movie theater in an old strip center. At least Vivienne thought it had been a theater. The marquee, if it had ever had one, had been removed, but the ticket office still faced the street, and the double doors reminded her of those that had graced the Durango. Miguel killed the engine and got a set of keys out of the seat divider. "It came on the market two days ago. Let's go take a look."

He got out of the truck and headed toward the door. Vivienne's head was spinning as she scrambled out of the truck. By the time she got across the sidewalk he had the theater's door open and had walked inside the gloomy lobby. He used a flashlight to find the light switch located behind the concessions counter. "The realtor said the electricity was still on."

He hit the switch and the deco-style light fixtures blazed. "Oh my God, it looks like the Durango," she breathed as she scanned the old lobby. The paint was gray and peeling and the carpet was water-stained and everything was covered with a thick layer of dust and grime. But the lobby's bones were good. The moldings were intact and the light fixtures all seemed to work.

"It should look like the Durango. Same architect and same builder. This one's a few years older and styled more along deco lines."

Vivienne took her time looking at the lobby. She checked out the area behind the counter and ran her finger across the molding as her mind raced. It would need a good scrubbing down. The walls would have to be sanded and painted. The carpet would have to be replaced. It would take a lot of elbow grease, but not all that much money for the lobby to be ready to go.

The lobby was doable.

Miguel waited patiently for her to finish her perusal, then ushered her into the theater, which was lit by only his flashlight. "I have to go upstairs to turn on the lights. Will you be all right down here in the dark?"

"I'm fine." She was trembling and her heart was beating in her throat, but never mind that.

Miguel disappeared and the theater was plunged into absolute darkness. Then she saw the bobbing of the flashlight beam in the balcony and suddenly the deco-style light fixtures along the walls winked on. The theater was more deep than wide, with long aisles stretching to an old-style screen that had faded to a dull gray.

Old-fashioned speakers hung from either side of the screen. She looked around for a moment before walking slowly down the aisle. The seat cushions were stained and dirty, but the old wood and iron seats appeared to be in good shape. As in the lobby, the walls could use some paint. A couple of the fixtures weren't working. She made her way to the front and climbed the side steps to the narrow stage. It was wider than it would be in a modern theater, but still too narrow for stage productions. She fingered the old curtains –filthy, but otherwise not too bad. Vivienne flicked on her cell phone flashlight and walked down the narrow passage between the old screen and the back wall of the theater, dodging the cobwebs and the support beams holding up the screen. Behind the screen she found more old-style speakers and a locked door she figured led to the alley outside.

As it was, it wouldn't be usable for live theater. But then, neither had the Durango when it was first built. With the right renovations, it could be everything the Durango had been.

Miguel was sitting in the front row. He patted the chair beside him, sending up a cloud of dust. She gave the dust a minute to disperse and sat down beside him. "Well, what do you think?" he asked.

"It would need some heavy renovations before it could be used for live theater."

"I realize that." He jumped up and paced off twenty-five or so feet. "Everything from here forward would have to be rebuilt. The screen taken down, the front rows of seats removed, the stage extended to about here." He motioned to a spot with his hand. "Dressing rooms and a backstage restroom would have to be added. Piece of cake for my crew. You, Josh, and Cameron could design it, and get what you want. Did you find the locked door? That leads to a big room that could be used for props and storage. Set pieces could be stored back there between uses. Offices could be in the vacant storefront on one side, and the Academy on the other. The entire block's for sale."

"The whole block?"

"With the caveat that the businesses renting the spaces be allowed to stay until their leases expire."

Vivienne looked around the old theater. It didn't look like much now. But with the right renovations, it would be perfect. "I don't know what to say. It would have been perfect a month ago. But the consortium's fallen apart. There's nobody to buy it now."

"That's where you're wrong." He sat down with one seat between them. "I could buy it, Vivi. You and the Durango bunch could have your theater and I could rent out the rest of the space."

Vivienne glanced over at Miguel. He had on his negotiating face again. "And?"

"You marry me again."

Vivienne sat back in the chair. She hadn't seen this coming. But she should have. He wouldn't have gone to this much trouble otherwise. "Miguel, I don't have much in the way of assets to bring this time around. You already have the all the social connections you need. And you wouldn't be getting a share of Heiser Steel. You don't need me."

Miguel lifted his eyebrow. "You're still Tripp Heiser's daughter. You own a multimillion-dollar business that's now on sound footing. If we had children, and this time around I want them, they would be Heisers, even if they do carry my name. Believe me, that's assets enough." He smiled sardonically. "And don't forget the sex."

"Heaven forbid we should forget the sex."

"Or the fun."

"Or the fun," she echoed softly.

She swallowed and looked around the theater. Tears stung her eyes. To get so close, and then have to turn it down. It would be so easy to say yes to him, to go back to what they'd had before. But she couldn't, even if it cost her the theater. He didn't love her and never would.

Tears welled in her eyes and she looked at him with a lead weight in her heart. "I... I can't," she whispered. "I want it so bad I can taste it, but I can't. I'm sorry." She groped for the words to make him understand. "It's not about money with me, even though you think it is. I want to marry for love. I want to marry a man who I love and who loves me back. You don't do love. To you it's all about assets." She looked at him with tears running down her cheeks. "I don't want it to be about assets, Miguel. I want it to be about love." She dashed the tears off her cheeks.

He stared at her for a long minute. "I guess that's it, then. Let's go." She watched as he jumped up and started up the aisle. He was about halfway to the door before he turned on his heel and faced her. "You know what, Vivi? This isn't it. *Hijo de puta*, woman, use your damned head." He stomped back down the aisle and gestured around the theater. "Do you really think I'd buy this rundown old place that's going to bleed money like a stuck pig every damned day I own it if I didn't love you? Do you really think I'd put one of my crews to work down here on my nickel if I didn't love you a whole hell of a lot?" He slammed his hands into his pockets. "And if you weren't so damned hardheaded, you could learn to love me, too." His anger faded and he looked at her like a teenage boy about to ask a girl to go out on a date. "I'm not so bad, you know."

Vivienne stared at him in shock. "You love me?"

"Yes, I love you." He sank down in the chair beside her.

"But you turned your nose up at the thought of marrying for love. You came out and told me you considered marriage an exchange of assets."

"You were calling off our engagement. I was hurt and I said things I shouldn't have. I'm an ass and I'm sorry."

"I'm sorry, too. I didn't mean to hurt you. And you're not bad at all, Mico. You're really quite wonderful."

He took her hand. "Thank you for thinking so. Do you think you could do it? Do you think you could learn to love me like I love you?"

"I fell in love already. Weeks ago. That's why I gave you the ring back that afternoon in the parking lot. Loving you and knowing you didn't love me was killing me."

Miguel froze. "Well, hell. You know, *querida*, we really need to work on the communication piece of our relationship."

"Right. We seem to suck in the communication department."

Vivienne looked at him and they started to laugh. And then they were in each other's arms, kissing wildly and clinging to each other. She should have known he loved her. It was in his kisses, and in his touch. It was in the way his eyes softened when he looked into hers.

They held onto one another for long moments in the dusty old theater. He finally pulled away and got out his phone, shooting off a quick text before putting the phone away and taking her by the hand. "I'd like it to be different this time," he said quietly. "I worked too damn much and delegated too little. I won't be making that mistake again. This time around, the marriage comes first."

"I made my mistakes, Mico. I spent way too much time at the theater. I neglected you and our marriage. I won't do it again."

"Vivi, I want you to do your shows. Those are important to you. I'll support you better this time."

"I'll still do them. but not as many. Besides, there are some roles I can't play if I'm stuck out to here." She held out her hand in front of her and grinned.

"Are you okay with kids?"

"Yours? Sure. But don't be surprised when I make you build them a stage in the nursery."

He laughed. "Fair enough." He took her hand and pulled her against him. She molded herself to his body and kissed him with everything she had. By the time they came up for air, her legs were wrapped around his waist, and her hands were under his shirt.

Gently, he lowered her to the floor, and then whispered in her ear, "I can't wait to get you home, *querida*."

They turned off the lights and walked into the lobby, then out into the hot May sunlight. And almost ran into a sturdy ladder propped against the building right in front of the door.

"What in the world?"

They ducked around the ladder and stood holding hands on the sidewalk.

Wade's truck was parked next to the curb, and Wade and a couple of Miguel's employees were securing the Durango Street Theatre marquee to the building. Vivienne let out a little squeal and threw her arms around Miguel's neck. "Oh my God. Look at that. The Durango's back. Thank you, thank you, thank you, Miguel. I love you so much."

"And I love you. Your wedding present, *querida*."

His kiss was long and lingering and accompanied by laughter and applause. Wade whistled and gave them a thumbs-up. "The theater's back and the Abonces are together again," he hollered. "From where I'm standing, it's a damn good day."

Vivienne and Miguel thought so, too.

Epilogue

Honestly. A wedding reception was not the place to have a shouting match.

On the other hand, it was a lot more entertaining than her sister's boring party going on inside.

Maggie Gutierrez sat down on the garden bench and kicked off her shoes. Kirby Martinez and his father were really going at it. "You don't give a damn, do you?" Kirby demanded. "You don't give a damn that the fucking police department falsely accused me of dealing drugs and let me swing in the wind for months to catch the real culprits. You could have hired a private detective and had my name cleared within a week. But no, you and your good buddy Ernest Navarro let me dangle for months in a bullshit plan to throw Misty and Alex together. You took advantage of the situation to play your fucking matchmaking games. And then you and your asshole friend had the gall to laugh about it. Shit, Dad. You *used* me."

Rolando Martinez laughed. "So? Your sister needed a husband and Ernest and I needed a way to get them together. It worked, didn't it? Misty's in there dancing with her husband. It was no big deal."

"No big deal? I was scared out of my mind for months. I couldn't eat. I couldn't sleep, thinking I was going to jail. All so you could get Misty a husband. I don't like being used."

"Tough shit. Your sister needed my help and I gave it to her. Get over it."

Rolando turned on his heel and sauntered away, apparently unaffected by their exchange. Kirby, not so much. He uttered a few choice curse words under his breath, and if the way he was swaying was any indication, he'd paid a few too many visits to the bar.

Not a smart thing for a recovering addict to do.

Maggie held her breath as he staggered toward the bench where she sat. He seemed oblivious to her presence until he stumbled over one of her shoes. "Crap. It's already taken," he said as he clutched the arm rest. "I'll find another."

"Looks to me like you better sit down before you fall down." She followed the comment with a soft giggle.

"Maggie?"

"In the flesh."

"Thanks for the invite." He flopped down on the bench. "I don't know where any more benches are."

"This one's plenty big for the both of us. Stay here until you sober up and get over being pissed."

Kirby glanced over at her. "You heard?"

"Loud and clear."

"Well, hell." He leaned forward and put his head in his hands.

She glanced at him, his hair a mess and his loose tie hanging unevenly. A couple of years older than Maggie, he was the child of Rolando, her mother Gladys's first husband, and a second wife who had died sometime back. Misty had been a baby when her parents divorced, and both Rolando and Gladys had made much happier second marriages. Maggie and Kirby were the product of those second marriages. Not related, but thrown together every now and again at family gatherings.

Considerably younger than the older sister they had in common, their paths had crossed a few times over the years, usually at celebrations for their sister. Kirby had grown from a skinny boy to a gangling teenager to a good-looking young man. Somewhere along the way Maggie had developed a crush on him, despite the fact that he had been spoiled rotten by his parents and had made some really stupid choices in the last few years that had come back to bite him in the butt. He'd always been nice to Maggie, and he'd been downright flirtatious last night at the rehearsal dinner, with smiles and little come-on looks, which had her blushing and flirting right back.

But he didn't appear to feel all that flirtatious now.

He turned to her, his eyes blazing. "So you heard. I can't believe what they did to me. And then laughed about it. I've never been so fucking angry in all my life."

"What were they laughing about?"

"How their little scheme had worked and that their fair-haired darlings had fallen in love. Dad never once thought about me or how I might have felt during all those months."

Maggie rolled her eyes. "I doubt that's true. Maybe he thought it would be good for you to sweat a little and think about some of the idiot choices you've made in the last couple of years. Like getting hooked on drugs. Or like seeing your drug-using buddies once you got out of rehab. Or maybe he was remembering all the worrying he did when you were using and how you needed to get back a little of your own."

"What? You're blaming me?" He looked at her, aghast. "Geez, Maggie, I thought you of all people would understand."

"I don't understand stupidity, especially avoidable stupidity like recreational drugs. As for thinking about you, it seems to me that's all your father has done in the twenty-two years since your birth. He's thought about you, he's done everything for you, he's spoiled you rotten to the point that you're furious that he put Misty first for once and did something at your expense to help your big sister. *Pobrecito* Kirby, he had to play second fiddle. *Dios,* Kirby, your father's neglected Misty most of her life. Is it really so awful that for once he did something for her?"

Kirby looked at her, incredulous. "He could have helped her without using me. Okay, I'm spoiled. I shouldn't have gotten started on drugs. I gave my father plenty to worry about. I admit all that and then some. But using me as a means to his end was still wrong, I don't care how spoiled and terrible I am." His hands clenched into fists. "You don't do that to people, Maggie. You don't use them, not if you're good and decent. You don't use them, you don't exploit them and you don't take advantage of what they can do for you. That's what they did to me."

"Tell me how you really feel." She couldn't quite stifle a snicker. After the shit he'd pulled, his indignation was hilarious.

"Go ahead and laugh if you want to. To me it's no laughing matter. And you know what? It stops with them. Nobody, and I mean nobody, ever better try to exploit me, take advantage of me, or use me again for as long as I live."

ABOUT THE AUTHOR

The author of over thirty romance novels, Emily Mims combined her writing career with a career in public education until leaving the classroom to write full time. The mother of two sons, she and her husband split their time between central Texas, eastern Tennessee, and Georgia visiting their kids and grandchildren. For relaxation Emily plays the piano, organ, dulcimer, and ukulele for two different performing groups, and even sings a little. She says, "I love to write romances because I believe in them. Romance happened to me and it can happen to any woman—if she'll just let it."

Connect with Emily:
facebook.com/emily.mims.756
twitter.com/emilymimsauthor
instagram.com/mims_emily
website: emilymims.com

www.BOROUGHSPUBLISHINGGROUP.com

If you enjoyed this book, please write a review. Our authors appreciate the feedback, and it helps future readers find books they love. We welcome your comments and invite you to send them to info@boroughspublishinggroup.com. Follow us on Facebook, Twitter and Instagram, and be sure to sign up for our newsletter for surprises and new releases from your favorite authors.

Are you an aspiring writer? Check out www.boroughspublishinggroup.com/submit and see if we can help you make your dreams come true.

www.ingramcontent.com/pod-product-compliance
Lightning Source LLC
Chambersburg PA
CBHW051820170626
46807CB00003B/949